FRIENDS
AND
CONSPIRATORS

FRIENDS
AND
CONSPIRATORS

Stephen Palmisano

Trafford rev. 10/12/2011

 www.trafford.com

North America & International
toll-free: 1 888 232 4444 (USA & Canada)
phone: 250 383 6864 ♦ fax: 812 355 4082

CONTENTS

INTRODUCTION

Harry Smith, Joe Cooper, and Dan Jones first met on the school bus, taking them to their first day in kindergarten. They were quite different from each other. Harry was much bigger, and quite a bit smarter than the other children that were his age. Joe was a very handsome young boy and very outgoing. Dan was very shy, and not very big for his age. The three young boys had very little in common, except for the invisible bond that drew them together, and made them friends. This bond grew stronger as time passed and made their friendship eternal.

Some of us go through life without ever having known a true friend, or finding a soul mate to share our joys and sorrows. Fortunate are those who have true friends, and are lucky enough to be married to their soul mate. The friendship of the three boys became so noticeable to the other children that they started to call them the three amigos.

Life has a habit of bringing the unexpected each day. Sometimes these unexpected events are very tragic. It's at these times that we seek the advice and support of those closest to us. Although the three friends in this novel chose different careers, they find ways to council each other when they are needed. When life brings tragedy to one of the trio, the two survivors find the way to solve the conspiracy that was plotted against them. They enlist the aid of a talented and trustworthy young man to help solve the clever plot of the conspirators to gain power. After an extensive investigation, the conspirators are unmasked, and brought to justice for their crimes.

Life's problems don't end with the resolution of one event. The unexpected seems to await it's next opportunity for evil to strike, but with good friends and trusted staff, the evil doers are brought to justice.

CHAPTER I

Terrible News

My name is Daniel Jones. I am the minister and pastor at Saint Paul's Anglican Church on the fringe of the very small town of Meadow Valley, Ohio. The population of our town never quite reached twenty thousand residents. There had never been more than one elementary, and one high school. Our business district, in the center of town was very small, but provided all the services that the town's residents required. My parents, grandparents, and I, have always lived here, and so did the ancestors of most of the town residents.

Meadow Valley was first settled by colonists who had completed their indentured servant requirements that had been mandated by courts in England, to satisfy their failure to pay their debts. These people had the choice to either go to debtors prison or be transported to the English colonies in America. These colonists took advantage of the land grants that were given by the English authorities wishing to extend their influence further west. Some of the buildings in the center of town, still exist to this day. Saint Paul's church sits on the same site as the original church, which was destroyed by fire about one hundred years ago. The rebuilt church resembles the original building, so I was told except for the rear meeting hall addition, which had been recently added.

I had just returned from Sunday services, after conducting the weekly sermon to my parishioners of my church. The sermon this Sunday was taken from the Gospel according to Saint Matthew, chapter five, verse one to twelve, the Lords sermon on the mount. As I sat there, I thought to myself, how joyful life could be if mankind would follow the guidance provided in the sermon. My wife Josie was busy preparing dinner while I read the newspaper, and reflecting back to my sermon. This was our usual quiet time after fulfilling the weekly duties of the ministry to my congregation. The telephone rang, and I grudgingly got up from my recliner chair to answer it. The call was from my older sister, who sounded quite upset, as she told me to turn on the television news for a special report. I asked her what was it about, but she said, "just turn on the news, and you will see". I hung up the phone as my wife questioned me on what was all the fuss about. The news on the television soon answered our question. There had been an assassination attempt on the President of our country. He had survived, but his trusted Advisor and close friend, who was traveling with him, was killed by coming between the President and the assassin. The details were still vague on the news report, but it was confirmed that my childhood friend, Harry Smith was dead. The President, Joe Cooper, his special Advisor, Harry Smith, and I had been close friends since our childhood. We first met in kindergarten, and the three of us were inseparable all the way through elementary, high school, and college. It was in college that all three of us met our wives. After graduation, we all three married these college girlfriends. Only then did we go our separate ways to pursue our different careers.

Joe Cooper went to law school for his post graduate studies. Harry Smith went to an architectural school, and received his license to practice architecture. I went to a theological seminary for my post graduate studies for my chosen career. Even though I had kept in touch with my two friends, it seemed so very long ago when we first met.

In college we belonged to the same fraternity, and our future wives belonged to the same sorority. Our wives first met each other in college, and have remained very close friends through the years.

We spent the whole day getting the latest news updates from the television. I tried to contact Harry's wife Sally, but was unable to even leave a message. My wife Josie, and I, felt sad and helpless at the news of the death of our friend, but there was nothing to be done except to wait for someone to contact us. That Sunday passed more slowly than any other day, that I can ever recall.

That next morning at breakfast, the phone rang. The call was from an executive aid to the President. He told me to hold on as the President would talk to me in a moment. Soon President Joe Cooper was on the phone with me. After our salutations, he told me how our friend Harry gave up his life to save him from the assassin. He then told me that Harry's wife Sally, wanted him buried in their family plot in our hometown cemetery. It was her desire that the wake and church services be held in the town where Harry came from. I was the only one of the three friends that was presently living in our town of Meadow Valley. Joe Cooper and Harry Smith still had homes on the outskirts of our town, but their duties to our government required them to reside in Washington. The President then told me that Harry's body would be sent to our town on Wednesday for the wake and the funeral services, and the burial would take place on Saturday. He and his wife Karen would arrive in Town on Thursday. Harry's wife Sally, and her son John would arrive in town on Wednesday afternoon. It's their wish that the funeral mass be held at your church, and that Harry's body lay in state at the church. It is also their wish that you give the eulogy for your friend as she was certain that Harry would want you to do this. He then told me that he would also like to say some words for his close friend.

Our church, Saint Paul's, wasn't very big, but it was still the largest church in our small town. I prayed that the weather would be nice enough to allow for the huge crowds of people who were sure to want to attend this service. The church could hold only so many, and the number of those wishing to express their sympathy was sure to be enormous. The plaza in front of our church was large, and could accommodate a large number of people. Speakers could be set up so that they could hear the service. Harry's body would be laid in state in our church so that those wishing to pay their respects could do so. Our towns funeral parlor was way too small to accommodate such a large number as would be expected to attend the funeral.

I thanked the President for his personal call, and assured him that I would do all that I could to properly send off our dear friend. My wife Josie waited till I had hung up the telephone before she asked me about the funeral plans. She said that Harry's wife, Sally, and their son John must be devastated at the death of their husband and father.

There had been rumors before this attempted assassination attempt on the President and death of Harry that Harry's son John and President Joe Cooper's daughter Susan, had been seen together quite frequently on dinner dates and on various other occasions. The media is always exaggerating any relationship theory, and, we didn't know if there was any truth to this gossip. I sat there contemplating what preparations that I would be required to start making, and what Josie and I could do on a personal level to ease the sadness that Harry's wife and son were enduring.

My wife, Josie, Harry's wife Sally, and President Joe Cooper's wife Karen, were sorority sister in college, and had always been very close friends. They had maintained their close friendship through the years, since their college days. Unlike some relationships between women, there had never been jealousy or rivalry between the three of them. This they had in common with their husbands, who also had been friends though the many years, without there ever having been any serious disputes between them. We three were like loving brothers that none of us had from our parents. The only one of us who had any siblings was myself who had one older sister.

I felt overwhelmed with the responsibility that lay ahead, but the sadness of losing my friend would help me do what had to be done for his sake, and for the sake of his wife and son.

CHAPTER II
Contemplation

I went over to the front window and looked out at the gently falling rain of this late April afternoon. As I stared at the rain splashing on the pavement, and observing the first signs of Spring life on the surrounding vegetation, I felt a calming relief to the tension brought on by the terrible news of my friend Harry's death. My thoughts then went to the many things that I must do in the next few days for my friends funeral. The President's and his wife's parents who lived out of town, would probably stay with the President at his home on the outskirts of our town. Harry's and his wife's parents would stay with Sally and her son, John at their home near town. Our small town had one very old and small hotel, and two small motels on the edge of town. These accommodations would be overwhelmed with the influx of people coming to town for the funeral. There was one upscale restaurant in the center of town, and one old style diner. There are two fast food hamburger diners on the edge of town. It was perplexing for me to wonder how this town could provide services for so many visitors. I thought that perhaps our high school gym might be used to accommodate some of the overnight visitors if that could be arranged. Thinking about all these logistical problems seemed to fill my thought, and I was at a loss to how these things could be resolved. I decided that I would contact the President to use his influence to solve these problems, and to send his representative to oversee the necessary preparations that would be required. My thoughts then went to what I would say for my friends eulogy. I started to think back to the time when we all three met for the first time in kindergarten. Joe Cooper was always the most outgoing and handsome one. Harry was our protector and always the tallest and biggest of our group. He was also the smartest, and our leader. I was the quiet one and very bashful as a child, and didn't come out of my self imposed shell until my junior year in high school. It was then that I started to have thoughts of becoming a minister. That is when I started to intently study the bible. I recall that Harry and Joe never ridiculed me for constantly carrying my pocket size bible, as some of the other kids did.

The country's economy was in shambles when Joe Cooper was elected to the Presidency of our nation. It was these hard times that was the reason for his success in defeating his opponent in the election. Harry and I, and our wives were Joe Cooper and his wife Karen's personal guests at his fist inauguration and all of the fancy inaugural balls that followed. Harry wasn't part of Joe Cooper's administration in his first two years in office. With President Joe Cooper's failure to fix the nations economy, and the dissatisfaction that he had with his political party's advisers, convinced the President to turn to his close friend Harry to come to Washington, to be his closest adviser.

With Harry's advice and ideas for various programs to create jobs, the country started to come out of the deep economic recession that it was in, and this guaranteed Joe Cooper's success in his election for his second term as President. This successful run for his second term was a very happy time for the three of us. With the positive outcome of last Novembers election completed, we all celebrated a very joyful holiday season here in town. The last time that Josie and I were in the company of Joe and Harry and their wives was at last January's inauguration for his second term. My thoughts went back to that day, and the evening inaugural balls that followed. That was a very pleasant and exciting experience for Josie and I. We were part of the Presidents personal entourage that made the rounds of the numerous balls and events that he was expected to attend. It was shortly after that day that the rumors in the media started to imply that the Presidents daughter Susan, and Harry's son John were an item. They were apparently dancing together too often and too close, and paying too much attention to each other, to escape the observation of the media, who were always quick to pick up on anything that might be gossip or newsworthy.

Joe, Harry, and I, were approximately the same age. We were all in our mid-fifties. Our wives were also the same age as us. John and Susan were in their early twenties, and both finished with college. What post graduate plans that they had were unknown to me, but I'm sure that they would both do well, because they both were very bright.

I turned on the television for the latest news updates on the assassination attempt. The assassin was killed by the President's bodyguards. It turned out that the authorities could not identify who this person was, or that he ever existed. His finger prints, and D.N.A gave no clue to who he was. He had nothing on him to aid in his identification. The autopsy that was yet to be done might give some clues to his identity, but as of now the police and F.B.I had nothing to go on for the assassins motive, or if there were others involved in this attempt to kill the President. This murderous act cost the President and I our close friend, and the nation a very smart and gifted adviser to the Presidency. I thought, how slim a thread determines the events of history. I switched over to the different television networks, but there was little to be gained in new developments on this tragedy.

I then wondered what I should say about my friend in the eulogy that was my responsibility to give. It bothered me quite a bit that I might not be up to the task. I wanted to tell the world how smart Harry was, and to tell everyone that the Presidents recent successes were due to the brilliance of his friend and adviser, but I dare not go there as it would be misinterpreted as a knock against the President by his political opponents. I must be very careful, so that I do no harm to my friend, Joe Cooper. I walked over to the front window again and noticed that the rain had stopped, and the sky had cleared. The sunshine gave a glow to the still wet pavement, and a rainbow appeared above. As I looked above at the rainbow, my thoughts went to the promise in the bible that the earth would not again be covered by flood waters. As I gazed at this scene, I said a silent prayer for inspiration and guidance for the tasks that lay before me.

I went back to my recliner chair and sat down to think about all the things that must be done in the next few days. Where shall I begin? I pondered over these tasks in my mind, but to no avail in relief of my tasks. I closed my eyes, and my thoughts went back to the day that all three of us met for the first time.

CHAPTER III

Friends Meet

It was two days after Labor Day, and the start of the new school year. My mother had me all ready to start school, and accompanied me to the front yard to await the arrival of the school bus. When the bus arrived, my mother had to literally force me to get on. I recall that I thought a hundred demons awaited me. Joe and Harry were already on the bus, and Harry who even then was larger than the other kids, noticed how scared I was. He came over to me like a loving older brother, and welcomed me into my new world of school. I sometimes wonder if he ever knew how much that meant to me. He sat down next to me, and then introduced me to Joe Cooper. By the time that the bus arrived at school my fears had subsided, and with my protector Harry at my side, and my new friend Joe, I started on this new phase of my life. When I came home that day my mother expected that my eyes would be swollen with tears, but was surprised to see how happy I was. My mother was wondering how my fear of school had ended so quickly. It was then that I told her about my new friends. I was eager to get on the school bus that next morning without any prodding from my mother. All three of us were five years old when we started kindergarten. Joe Cooper was big for his age and socially advanced beyond the other kids except Harry. Harry was far ahead of all of us in his development, and he was also much bigger. He could have very easily skipped kindergarten and first grade and gone directly into second grade, and he might even surpass them in intellect. I was on par with the other kids in kindergarten, but my new found friends made me feel very happy and secure. How lucky I felt to have two wonderful friends. My shyness and bashfulness would probably have been a huge problem for me except for them. Harry was always the peacemaker in any of the disputes between any of our classmates, but never the bully. Even at that early age I could tell that our teacher had noticed Harry's leadership and kindness. I heard her comment many times how smart and well behaved he was. Our teachers took advantage of Harry's and Joe's leadership qualities in the school days that followed, and our whole class was the beneficiary of their presence. Having Harry and Joe in our class was such as asset for our teachers that they were able to advance the curriculum for the whole class. This was pointed out by the teachers and many of the parents of my classmates. At the end of the school year the kindergarten children graduated on stage in the school auditorium, wearing caps and gowns. It was on this occasion that I witnessed for the first time that Harry felt uncomfortable. He was aware that he was much bigger then the other children and that he looked out of place in this group.

Summer vacation came and we three didn't see each other as much as when we were in school, but as the end of summer neared, Harry and Joe would walk over to my house for some play time.

When school started I was eager to get back to the routine of school work. One of the boy's father in our first grade class was coaching a little league football team. Harry, Joe, and I were eager and excited to participate in the new undertaking. Our enthusiasm didn't last very long because of the obvious and constant favoritism shown by the coach to his son. Because of Harry's size and superior athletic ability, he was excluded from most of the practice by the coach, with the excuse that he might injure the other boys. Harry would sit on the bench with a very rejected look on his face while the rest of us were participating. This was the second time that I noticed how sad and disturbed that Harry looked. Joe noticed this also and made an issue of this exclusion of Harry in the football activities with the coach. He told the coach that if Harry was not allowed to play with the rest of us that he would quit the team. This gave me the courage to also stand up for my friend. That was the last day that we played for that coach.

Elementary school years came and went so swiftly, mainly because of the many happy times that I spent with my two friends. We were called the three amigos by other classmates who saw what close friends we were. Harry was always the smartest kid in class, and he continued to be the biggest. Joe was the most popular, especially with the girls because of his good looks and outgoing personality. I continued to be shy and not very outgoing with others. At the end of our eighth grade, Joe was elected to be class president. Harry was voted to be most likely to succeed, and I was chosen to be class profit. It was my duty as class profit to write something about each of my classmates, and to give a speech at the class picnic. Before I gave this speech I fell into a stream at the picnic grounds and my carefully prepared notes written with soluble pen became illegible. I was forced to give my speech from memory. This was no small feat for a shy boy. With my teachers insistence and with Harry's and Joe's encouragement, I managed to complete my task. I remember that I prophesied that Joe would be our states Governor, and Harry would be a wealthy business man.

That summer we decided to give sports another try, and joined a little league baseball team. Joe was the pitcher and Harry was the catcher on this team. I played center field because of the only talent that I seemed to possess was my running speed. Playing baseball together on that team made for a very happy and quickly passing summer.

With the start of our freshman year in high school, all three of us entered into a new phase in our lives, as do all fourteen year old's. We were very excited to get started in the right of passage. Our boyish voices were gone, and our interests in cars and the opposite sex followed suit. We all three decided to try out for the junior varsity football team at school. All of us made the team. Joe was the quarterback, Harry was the running back and because of my running speed, I was the wide receiver. We had played only one opponent when Harry was sent to the varsity football team because of his obvious ability and talent. Soon Joe was also called up to play on the varsity team when the varsity quarterback was injured, and they needed a replacement for the back up quarterback who took over the first string job. Joe quickly was promoted to the string quarterback job with Harry at his side in the backfield as starting running back. This was quite a feat for two freshman. I continued to play on the junior varsity team, but was determined to make the varsity team next year so that I could join my friends. Reflecting back in time like this also reminded me of our first day in high school at lunch in the school cafeteria. I had just brought my lunch tray to a table, and as I sat down to wait for Joe and Harry to join me, a huge senior came over to me and slapped me on the side of the head, and said, "move squirt". Just as I was about to engage my protagonist, Harry arrived and gave this bully a push that sent him flying. He then calmly walked over to him and challenged him to do something about it. The bully took one look at the determined look on Harry's face and his large size, and meekly backed off. No bully ever threatened me or Joe in high school after that incident.

Our sophomore year in high school came and I finally made the varsity football team although, I spent most of the time sitting on the bench, cheering on my two friends. In my junior year on the football team, I started to get more playing time, and with my very fast running speed, I was able to contribute to the team. My association with Joe and Harry finally made my shyness fade and gave me the courage to come out of my shell, and become more outgoing. Time passed so quickly, and soon the end of high school was near. Many people think back to their high school years as a very traumatic time in their lives, but for me these were very happy years because of my friendship with Joe and Harry. At high school graduation I felt very sad because I felt that my close association with my two friends was about to come to an end. Harry took both Joe and me aside as we were about to leave the ceremony, and told us to convince our parents to enroll us in our state college so that we could continue our education together. With unanimous agreement we vowed to make this happen. Our college years went by swiftly, and even though we didn't have many classes together, we still saw each other often because we all belonged to the same fraternity, and because we all played school sports together. Joe and Harry were standouts on the football and baseball teams. I also played on both of these teams, but I never had the athletic ability of my two friends. My running speed, however served me well in these sports. Our future wives to be were sorority sisters at our college, and also they all were cheerleaders. This is how we met them. We dated them all through our college years, and they became an integral part of the three amigos. At the end of college we all three married these college sweethearts, and went out separate ways to continue on with our post graduate studies for our chosen careers. We did however reunite at each of our wedding where we stood up for each other at the ceremonies. We all three had small inexpensive weddings because none of us, or our parents were very flushed with money after the expenses of college. None of us seemed to mind that we didn't have big wedding bashes as long as we could have our close friends with us on this special day.

CHAPTER IV
Our Careers

Joe went to law school, and with his handsome looks, and excellent personality, and intellect, was sure to be very successful at this profession. After his law school studies were completed and his bar exams passed, Joe took a position in the State Attorney General office. He quickly advanced up the ladder to higher positions, and ultimately was first appointed and then elected to be our States Attorney General. After serving notably in this elected office for two terms, he was selected to run for Lieutenant Governor on his political parties ballet in the coming election. With a successful outcome in this election, he served in this position for almost two full terms. Towards the end of the Governors second term, he had an unexpected heart attack which caused his death, and Joe Cooper became our States Governor. In the subsequent election that followed, he was easily elected because of his excellent credentials and superb performance as acting Governor. This elected office ultimately led to his being selected by his political party to be their candidate to run for President of the United States. The very bad economy in the nation at the time of this election, facilitated him in defeating his incumbent opponent. Joe's political party was initially favoring a U.S. Senator named Andrew Walker to be their candidate, but had to select a compromise candidate when a stalmate arose at the convention between Walker and another U.S. Senator. His party then chose Andrew Walker to be the Vice President on this ticket.

Harry's post graduate studies were at an architectural school. With his intellect and innovative ideas, he was sure to excel in this field. After he finished his studies, he proved this by his swift advancement in a large architectural firm, and by the beautiful buildings that he designed. Harry left this firm to start his own company, and very soon he was becoming very wealthy. Harry was recognized for his accomplishments by his peers by giving him their annual award for excellence for his work which was well deserved. Harry only temporarily left his profession because of the Presidents request, and urgent need for a trusted adviser. President Joe Cooper knew that he with the help of his friend could bring the nation out of these hard times. The President felt that he and Harry could accomplish anything.

I went on to a theological college for my post graduate studies. When my graduate work was completed, I was appointed to be the assistant to the Pastor of Saint Paul's Church, here in my home town. The pastor being quite on in years needed someone to help him with the ministry of this parish. I elevated to his job as pastor when he retired. My life and chosen career was uneventful in comparison to my two friends, but very happy and fulfilling, none the less.

CHAPTER V

Funeral Preparations

All of a sudden I felt a nudge on my shoulder. My wife said; "you have been sitting in that chair, in a trance for quite a long time,. What are you thinking about"? I responded that I was just reminiscing back in time to the days when I first met Joe and Harry, and our time in high school together. Josie gave me a look that let me know that she understood the sadness that I was feeling for the loss of my friend. She then told me that dinner was almost ready. I got up from my chair and walked over to the front window and watched as the mix of sun and rain each took their turn. It was still light outside. The daylight hours were getting longer, but the sunlight shadows were different from my observations earlier in the day.

Josie called, "dinner is ready" and I went to the kitchen to join her. After dinner was finished I told her that I better write the eulogy for Harry's funeral mass before the evening was over because there would be little time to do this on the following days with all of the other preparations that are needed. Josie told me to call the telephone number that the President gave to me to get assistance from the government for the funeral before I did anything else. Josie poured us coffee, and after I finished it, I made the call to ask for assistance, but was unable to get through.

After failing in this I went to my study and sat down at my desk to compose the eulogy for my friend. I don't know why I was experiencing so much difficulty with this task, but it was very hard for me to be satisfied that I did it right. I finished the eulogy at about ten P.M. And then went to the living room where Josie sat watching television. At eleven P.M. The evening news came on with the latest updates on the assassination attempt. It had been a full day and a half and still no new developments were known or being reported. The assassin's identity was still eluding the investigators. After the news we both went to bed.

Tuesday morning arrived, and after breakfast I placed another call to Washington to get help for the funeral preparations. This time the contact number given to me by the President got quick results, and I was assured that help would arrive in town on Wednesday morning. Harry's body and his family were scheduled to arrive in town on Wednesday afternoon. I decided to get as much done as I could before help arrived. I knew that Harry's family had a burial plot in our local cemetery, as did both the President and my family. This cemetery was on the outskirts of town, and there was plenty of rural space nearby. After the church service, and the trip to the cemetery there would be a need for someplace to hold the traditional funeral breakfast. I thought that a huge tent could be set up on the rural space adjacent to the cemetery for this as there wasn't any facility in our small town large enough to accommodate this gathering.

I didn't want to presume too much without the permission of Harry's family, so I placed a call to Harry's son John with the hope of getting through to him, but was only able to leave a message for him to return my call. I decided to make a list of all the things that I could think of starting with the tent, caterers for the breakfast, calling our local funeral director to make arrangements for the burial, flowers, trip from church to the cemetery, rest room facilities at the breakfast, parking, and arrangements for the media at church and at the breakfast. It was my intention to give the list to the person that the President was sending from Washington to handle the burial. I placed a call to our local and only funeral director to alert him of our intention for the burial with the information that I had at this time. I told him that I would call back when I knew more. Shortly after this call, Harry's son returned my call. After I expressed my deepest sympathy for his loss, I told him of my call from the President, and his instructions for the burial. I wanted to know if he and his mother were ok with me proceeding with the arrangements. He advised me that he had already spoken to the President about the arrangements, and he and his mother were grateful that the President and I were taking care of things. John told me that there was only a minimal autopsy performed on Harry's body to retrieve the bullet that killed him and to establish the cause of death. Harry's body would be embalmed in Washington and the casket selected there. His body would go directly to my church to lay in state. John confirmed that he and his mother and Harry's body would arrive in town on Wednesday afternoon. He also told me that the President's aid would be sent to town to handle the arrangement with me.

After my call from Harry's son John, I called the funeral director to advise him of the latest information. When my call to the funeral director ended I sat there at my desk wondering what I forgot to think of. I knew that our small town would be overwhelmed with visitors seeking overnight accommodations. Perhaps the President's aid could use his influence to use our school gym for this if necessary. I couldn't think of any solution to this problem, and the additional security that will be required to control the large influx of visitors. The Presidents aid will have to provide the security to insure that things go smoothly. Those wishing to stay overnight will have to bring their own accommodations.

I went over everything that I could think of on my list of preparations. I asked my wife to check my list to see if I forgot anything. Josie looked over my list and said the only thing that she could think of was that perhaps Harry's wife Sally, might like to have memorial cards printed up. She said that I should remind the aid to arrange for them.

The day passed slowly, and the anxiety of my responsibilities weighed heavily on me. There were few new developments on the news of the attempted assassination of the President and the murder of Harry. The news kept repeating the same things over and over, trying to put their own spin on things, I didn't sleep very good that night because of all the things that must be done in the next few days. I just hoped that everything would go smoothly for the sake of my friend and his family. Wednesday morning arrived, and I was up earlier than usual because of my eagerness to get everything settled. It was just before ten A.M. When three black SUV's drove up to the front of the church. Our home was next to the church so it didn't take but a minute for me to go out and greet them. The President's aid had spoken to on the phone introduced himself and the others in his party to me. His name was Jim Kelly. There was a total of twelve people in his group, and I invited all of them into our home for coffee. As Josie seated our guests and served coffee and refreshments, Jim explained the functions of those in his group. I gave him the list of things that I thought needed to be done to prepare for the funeral, and told him what I had already done. He thanked me and said that it was very helpful, and his people would pick up the ball from here. When we finished our coffee and snacks, I escorted Jim and the others to the church. They looked over everything very carefully, and asked me if it was ok to use the rear church hall for their base of operations and for their overnight accommodations. I said it would be fine, and he responded that the hall would provide all the space that they needed for their equipment. With this done I left Jim with his tasks, and went back to my house with a sense of relief that all was in good hands. When I got back, Josie told me to return a call to the funeral director. I immediately did so, and advised him that the President's staff was taking care of everything except for the limousines for the families trip from the church to the cemetery, and the Hearse to bring the casket, and the burial at the cemetery. I also gave him Jim Kelly' s phone number, and suggested that he call him to set up a meeting with him as soon as possible. It was about three P.M. When a motorcade drove up to the church to bring Harry's body. Jim Kelly saw to it that the casket was brought into the church, and directed its placement. His staff would provide security on a continuous basis. I watched as this was being done, and after just a few minutes Harry's son John came into the church. Jim and I both greeted him, and it was obvious that they knew each other. He told us that his mother and all of their parents had been taken to their town home, and that they would all come to the church that evening for a private showing for just the family and closest friends. I again expressed my sympathy to him on the death of his father. He told me that he knew of the close friendship with his father, and he was aware of how sad that both the President and I were. Josie came to the church and we both stayed with John until he returned to his home. It was evident to Josie and I that John was having a hard time dealing with this tragedy. It was seven thirty when John and his mother Sally, and their parents returned to the church. Josie and Sally hugged and the tears flowed profusely amongst all. It was very hard for all of us to come to grips with the fact that such a big, strong, and young person like Harry was dead. Seeing Harry lying there in the casket seemed so unreal to me. During the many years of my ministry at Saint Paul's Church, I have conducted the funeral services for many of my parishioners. It was always a very sad occasion for the family of the deceased, but always seemed more so when the dead person was young. I walked over to the coffin, and gazed into Harry's face. He looked so calm and reassuring, just as he always did in life. He looked like he could wake up from a sleep and jump out of the coffin, and take charge as he always did. I looked up from Harry's face and glanced over to John. He looked more like his mother Sally, but still had some of Harry's facial mannerisms. John looked back at me and without a word passing between us, we both knew of the grief that we shared. I looked back into Harry's face, and the thought then came to me how much the President would miss his friend and trusted adviser. The thought then came to me that in addition to the loss of advice to the nation from this very talented man, the field of architecture would also be denied the many beautiful buildings that never would be constructed because of Harry's premature death. His short life had accomplished much, but he still had so much more to offer the world. A tragedy indeed!

At about nine thirty, I directed some prayers, and after more expressions of sadness by all, we bid our farewells for the evening. Jim Kelly then told everyone that the visiting hours should be restricted to two to four P.M. And seven to nine thirty P.M. On Thursday and on Friday the visiting hours would be all day from ten A.M. To nine P.M. To allow for the many persons that are expected to pay their respects. These people will be ushered past the coffin in single file by my staff. The burial will take place on Saturday morning, after funeral services here in church. We all then left the church except for the security guards who would maintain twenty four hour guard duty.

CHAPTER VI

The President Arrives

The alarm clock sounded as I lay there in bed. I was wide awake and thinking about all of the days activities that lay ahead. I opened my eyes and realized that my wife was already up. It was then that I heard her movements in the kitchen. I glanced over to the window, and noticed that the light coming into the bedroom was diffused, letting me know that Thursday's weather would be cloudy with probably more Spring rain. The weather reports from last nights news had predicted this, but had also predicted that Friday through Sunday would be pleasant and sunny. I turned away from the window, and closed my eyes. My thought went over to the church where Harry's body lay in his coffin. Again I thought how young and strong he looked. So many times when I conducted the funeral mass for the dead, I would try to give support to their family and friends. I often wondered if my sermon made their sadness less painful. Thinking about Harry, taken from us before his time made me think about the many times that I presided at the funeral mass for the young who also died in their prime of life. Was there anything that could be done or said that would lesson the sorrow for the loss of a child or young person. The sermon that pointed out that there was a time to be born and a time to die didn't seem appropriate for those taken from us so young. No words could make sense of these passings.

Harry's best and most productive years were yet to come. He had already achieved many accomplishments in architecture and after his service to the President was no longer required, he would continue to exhibit his talent and brilliance in architecture. What a great loss I thought, and what a tragedy for his wife and son.

I got out of bed and went to the bathroom to shower and dress. When I went into the kitchen, Josie had my morning coffee waiting for me. As we both sat there at the kitchen table, she told me how bad she felt for Sally and her son. She said that she felt helpless, and was at a loss of what to say to her friend. I tried to comfort her, but there isn't any thing that can be done at times like this except to let them know of your love and support. I told her that we all should be proud that Harry gave his life for his friend and country.

Josie then prepared a light breakfast for us, and then I went over to the church. Jim Kelly was there with two of the security guards. I asked him if he or his men required anything, and he responded that they had everything that they needed. There were two large motor homes in the parking lot behind the church hall. The church hall and the motor homes were providing everything that they needed.

I went over to the casket and said a silent prayer for my friend, and then returned to my home. Josie said that while I was gone there was a call from the

President's office, and said that he will arrive in town shortly, and after going to their home would come to the church at about three P.M.. The Presidents aid also advised that prior to the Presidents arrival, the secret service would send a team of agents to the church to conduct a security check of the church and grounds, which is part of their normal standard procedure.

It was just after lunch when the Presidents security people arrived at the church. They conferred with Jim Kelly, and his staff, and then went about their assignments. Two of them came to our front door, and requested that they be permitted to look around our home. I of course welcomed them into our home, and they asked me if I owned any firearms, and I told them no. Josie asked me when they left if their checking of our home was necessary. I told her that I thought that this was standard procedure to check in advance where ever the President goes anywhere, especially now that an assassination has been attempted. I turned on the radio to see if there was any new developments in the case, but still there was no new news. It was shortly after three P.M. When the Presidents motorcade arrived at the church. President Joe Cooper, his wife Karen, and daughter Susan, accompanied by more secret service agents, went directly to the church where they were met by Jim Kelly and the other agents. Josie and I immediately went to the church to greet them. Josie and Karen embraced each other, first with smiles and then followed by tears as they reminisced and then talked about this tragedy. Joe and I shook hands and then hugged, each of us knowing the sorrow that we both felt at the passing of our friend. We walked over to the coffin and gazed at Harry lying there looking so reassuring and strong. He was always our protector. It just seemed so hard to accept the fact that he was dead. What can anyone say at a time like this that expresses the sentiment that we are feeling. Just then Harry;s son John arrived in church. He was greeted by all, and given their sympathy for his loss. He told us that his mother had taken ill, but would be at the church for the evening service. Susan went over to John and as they took each others hands and then hugged, showed their close feelings towards each other. After we all conversed for about an hour, I led those present in prayers for our departed friend, and told all that visiting hours would resume at seven P.M. As we were leaving the church, Joe Cooper asked me to ride back to their country home with him. He wanted to discuss some things with me. His wife Karen then asked Josie to also come so that they could catch up on things. We of course agreed, and drove back to their home with them.

Meadow Valley had not ever seen this much activity and influx of media and political celebrities that were now beginning to converge on our small town. It was very fortunate that Jim Kelly was there to take charge of all the things required for the funeral, and all the logistics, and arrangements for this influx of people. My early thoughts of pre-planning would be inadequate for the actual requirements necessary for Harry's funeral to run smoothly. At Joe Cooper's country home we were greeted by Karen's and Joe's parents who had recently arrived. Josie went off with Karen and the others, and I was asked by Joe to accompany him to his private study, When we entered the room, Joe shut the door, and asked me to have a seat close to his desk. In a low and somewhat secretive manner, he told me that before Harry's death, he and Harry had suspected a conspiracy against his presidency, coming from the highest levels of government, He then told me that now that Harry is gone, he didn't know who he could trust. He then said "I don't have a single bit of substantive evidence, but both Harry and I suspected that the Vice President, Andrew Walker, was somehow involved, and had knowledge of who was behind all this intrigue. The President then told me of the stalemate at the political convention when he was selected to be his parties candidate for president, and of the disappointment that then, Senator Andrew Walker felt because he was sure that he would get the nomination from the party to be their candidate. Joe then related the following; "After winning the election for my first term, I could always sense that Andrew Walker wasn't satisfied with only being Vice President, and never felt that I could trust and rely on him or any of the inner circle of politicians that seemed to be in his clique. After the first two years of my first term in office, it was evident to me that we were at cross purposes, and the country was suffering because we were not solving any of the huge economic problems that our country was going through. That's why I turned to Harry, and asked him to take an extended leave from his architectural business, and come to Washington to be my personal adviser. I don't have to tell you Dan, how smart and talented Harry was. You and I both know that he was always the smartest person that we knew, including the both of us. As a friend and patriotic citizen, Harry left his very profitable business to come to my aid. All of the reforms and initiatives that followed, in spite of the stiff opposition from those that had their own agenda, slowly but surely started to bring our country out of its economic woes. Some of the legislation that I was able to get through Congress were my ideas, and some were Harry's, and some were ideas that we worked on together, but without Harry's help I very much doubt that I would have been able to be successful at this undertaking."

The President then described the legislation that he and Harry were able to pass to solve the nations problems. The huge foreign trade deficit, the bank failures, the massive unemployment, the the housing foreclosures, the lack of medical availability for the uninsured, the lack of consumer confidence, these were all problems that the nation had to solve very quickly to avoid a deep recession. The President's plan for each of these problems was then described to me in detail.

The large number of bank failures that were presently occurring tn the nation were threatening to overwhelm the F.D.I.C.. To put an end to these failures, Harry and I put our heads together an drafted legislation to stop the excess profit taking, salaries, and bonuses, that banking officials were manipulating by unethical practices with their board of directors whom they appointed. This was a conflict of interest, and was resolved by this legislation that added taxes and penalties that put a stop to this. In addition to that problem we also put a stop to giving unsecured loans that were risky. We then put a stop to selling off these loans to third parties. With the banking controls put into law, the bank failures soon started to stop, and the banks started to make a fair profit for the stock holders and the companies.

The quality of health care in the country was excellent for those who could afford it. The problem was that too many couldn't afford the quickly rising cost of medical insurance. The enactment of socialized medicine would bankrupt the economy and result in a reduction in quality medical care. By the passing of tort reform legislation we were able to eliminate the excess profits by the legal profession, reduce the hospital and doctors insurance, and eliminate unnecessary medical tests that were performed only for avoiding lawsuits. We established a fair market value for all medical procedures and drugs, similar to the Japanese model of price controls. The legislation also limited the interference of Federal, State, and Local Government on the daily operations of hospitals and medical professionals. These agencies would now limit their function to insuring that hospitals and doctors operate in a safe and sanitary manner. There were also provisions in this new law to stop the A.M.A. From its negative practices of manipulating medical school enrollments to create shortage of professionals. Finally we added a provision similar to the old Hill-Burton law that funded the construction of new cost efficient hospitals. All of these changes were to have the effect of lowering the overall cost of health care, and allow free capitalistic enterprise to make it possible for all to afford health care, and allow free capitalistic enterprise to make it possible for all to afford medical insurance ecvept the very poor who would be subsidized by the Federal Government.

The very high rate of unemployment in the country was a problem that when solved would also restore the lack of consumer confidence that was a product of the bad economy. Jobs needed to be restored and new jobs created. The solution to this problem was a multifaceted approach. The first phase of this job creation was to provide seed money from the Federal Government to each of the fifty states, to hire architectural firms within their state to collaborate on planning for a new town to be built in each state. These completely new towns would each be a research model for minimal use of energy, and the development of futuristic living practices. Each town would get a fully funded seed project, such as a scientific research laboratory building, medical college, technical school, research center for recycling waste products, or research laboratory building for exploring new alternative energy concepts, or other facility appropriate to the formation of a new futuristic town. The least populated states would get a town designed to accommodate three thousand people. The towns for the mid-sized states would be designed for five thousand people, and the towns for the larger states would be designed for ten thousand. The infrastructure for all of these new towns would be funded by both the federal government and the state. This would include roads, bridges, and utilities. The funded seed project for each of these new towns would be the justification for the existence, stability, and growth of the towns. As the President described this idea that Harry and he came up with, he was very enthusiastic, and was convinced that these new towns would create numerous jobs, and the best new concepts for the future. The second phase of this job creation initiative was to closely monitor our foreign trade commitments to make sure that unfair practices were eliminated. To further enhance our countries manufacturing jobs, legislation was encouraged by us to have the federal, state, and local governments, purchase only goods produced in the U.S.A.. We also gave our support to legislation that gave tax incentives to companies that would stop outsourcing jobs to foreign countries. Our membership in the W,T,O, prohibited our country from placing protective tariffs on imported goods, so we were unable to put a stop to these imports that took away our jobs. The third phase for job creation was to have federal, state, and local governments come together to formulate a master plan for funding, planning, and reconstruction of our nations infrastructure, so that our roads, bridges, railroads, and dams are safe and maintained. The fourth phase of Harry's and my plan for job creation was to request the top management of professional sport teams in football, baseball, hockey, and basketball to come to Washington to meet with us, and hear our ideas. Our plan was to persuade them to visibly increase the size of their player rosters, and practice squads. The money from these larger rosters would come from salary caps on the high paid star players, and standard minimum pay scales for mostly inactive players, and graduated pay scales for active players. The other part of this initiative was to have each team have a farm club system of triple A, and double A, sport teams that they sponsor, and our associated with. These professional leagues were also encouraged to expand their franchises to as many new cities as possible. There was a definite desire by investors in many cities to be part of these leagues. Harry and I envision that this expansion of sports in our country will also create many jobs in related fields, such as sports medicine, coaching, physical training, and construction jobs for building, servicing, and maintaining these facilities. The next phase of our plan to get our country back on it's feet was to solve the housing foreclosure problem. We came up with a plan with the banks to renegotiate these bad loans for lower fixed rate loans with extension of mortgage length so that payments would be lower, and enable some of these homeowners to stay in their homes and avoid foreclosure. The government would guarantee that the banks wouldn't lose any more money on each loan than if the foreclosure had gone through. Both Harry and I were in agreement on all of these initiatives, and they were instituted as quickly as possible. As you know Dan, I signed all the legislation necessary to get things going, and as these programs came on line the country's economy quickly came out of the deep recession. While these plans to get our nation back on its feet were being implemented I could sense the disappointment displayed by the Vice President. With each positive outcome realized by the nations economy brought on by these programs enacted by Harry and I, Andrew Walker's demeanor became more hostile. It became very obvious that the Vice President and I were in for showdown. The nation gradually regained a positive attitude as the economy improved, and after two years of this economic recovery, my election to a second term as President was guaranteed. I was forced to retain Walker as my V.P. by our political party. He still had a substantial amount of power in the party. My attempt to replace Walker as my running mate has made him a bitter enemy. This is why I feel that he is at the bottom of this attempt on my life and the murder of our friend. I know that Andrew Walker felt that he should have been our parties candidate for president in my first term, and I feel that he would stop at nothing to get rid of me, and ascend to the presidency. Harry was my only trusted adviser. The Vice President has his tentacles of influence in every department of government, and I don't know who I can trust. That is why I asked Harry to give up his business and come to Washington, which has resulted in his death, and that is why I now ask you Dan, to take leave of your ministry, and come to Washington as my adviser. Dan; I need a trusted friend to be at my side, even if it's only for a short time, or until this conspiracy is solved. Asking you to leave your ministry at St. Paul's is asking quite a lot, but I desperately need someone I can trust to help guide me through this difficult time. After what has happened to Harry, this might be a very dangerous undertaking for you. Please think this over.

I told the president that I of course would go to Washington as soon as the Bishop provided a temporary replacement for St. Paul's. Joe responded that he would contact the Bishop to facilitate this. Just then, a knock on the door from Joe's daughter Susan, summoned us to join the others in the dining room for coffee. After a short time visiting with everyone, I told the President that we had to get back to the church, and prepare for the evening visiting hours. The President then summoned an agent to drive us back to our home. On the way home I told Josie of the presidents request for us to go to Washington. She was quite surprised at this prospect, and I am sure that numerous questions would follow as soon as the shock of all this wore off.

CHAPTER VII

THE FUNERAL

Visiting hours for those wishing to pay their respects to Harry's family were from seven P.M. to nine-thirty P.M. on Thursday, and on Friday they would be from ten A.M. to nine P.M.. The funeral service was set to start at nine A.M. on Saturday, with the breakfast to take place directly after the burial. Those coming to the church to pay their respects on Thursday were mostly the many friends of Harry and his family from our town. On Friday the influx of media and those coming from out of town was escalating as the day progressed. Jim Kelly, and his staff, handled the crowds with skill and expertise, and he assured me that all was taken care of for Saturday's funeral services, and the following breakfast. Harry's wife Sally, and son John, received those paying their respects for the entire time on Friday, only taking breaks, and standing in for each other when needed. The stress that they were under was visibly apparent on each of them as the hours went by. My wife, and the Presidents wife, sat by Sally, for most of the time to lend their support, and in some way try to ease her mourning.

It was about eight P.M. when the Vise President, his wife, and his group of associates, and security guards arrived at the church to pay their respects. After my conversation with the President on the previous day, I was intrigued by the absence of any indication of guilt on his face or in his demeanor. If the Presidents suspicions were true, his behavior did not show any indication that he was involved. He was either a very good actor or very clever. He was not to be underestimated.

Our small town was packed to the gills that Friday. Cars and motor homes were parked everywhere, as they were the only source of accommodations for those coming from out of town. Our few hotel rooms and eating establishments were filled to the maximum. In spite of this great number of out of town guests coming to the funeral, everything was running smoothly. The smallest details were all handled with expertise by Jim Kelly. I mentioned this to the President, and told him that in my opinion, he was very competent, and should be considered for advancement.

At about fifteen minutes to nine P.M., I directed those in the church at the time, in prayers for Harry, and told them that services would resume at nine A.M. on Saturday. Jim Kelly then assisted in making sure that everyone departed the church, and offered help as needed. This was greatly appreciated by Harry's family who were very tired from the long day that they had spent at the church. We all quickly paid our respects to Sally, John, and the others, and told all that we would meet at church on the following morning.

That evening, Josie questioned me why the President wanted us to go to Washington. I decided not to worry her, and told her that the President just needed a trusted opinion on some issues that he was facing, and that this move would only keep us in Washington for a couple of months. Josie then asked where we would stay? I responded that I was sure that the President will take care of all the details and expenses for this move. The President knows that our resources are limited. I then reminded her that we must wait for the Bishop to send a substitute to take care of the parish in our absence. I don't think that my explanations of why we were wanted in Washington were enough to satisfy her curiosity. The disturbed look on her face confirmed my suspicions, but it was best that she be told as little as possible about the dangers that we might face. Josie then said that it would be nice to have some idea of how long we would be in Washington so that she would know how much to pack. I told her to assume that we would only be gone a couple of months, and if we needed to bring more we could worry about that later. That night in bed, Josie was very restless.

Saturday morning arrived, and both Josie and I were up very early, and readied ourselves for the busy day ahead. At our light breakfast, I went over my notes for Harry's eulogy. At about eight A.M., both Josie and I went next door to the church. Jim Kelly was already there with all of his security guards.

I went over to him, and asked if everything was ready for the service and trip to the cemetary, and breakfast. "Everything is taken care of", he responded. As the time approached nineA.M., the church started to fill up. Harry's wife, Sally, and son John, arrived with the President, and his family. Soon the Vice President arrived with his group. By nine A.M. the church was packed. Jim Kelly had the T.V. networks choose one camera crew to film the event, with an agreement to all share this televising. This was necessary because of the limited space available. He also had microphones set up so that the crowds outside in the plaza in front of the church could hear the service. At a minute or two after nine everyone was seated, and I promptly began the service for my friend. At the conclusion of the service I went over to the pulpit, and took out my notes for the eulogy that I was about to give. For some reason I felt nervous, even though I had conducted this type of service many times. I suppose this was so because of my close friendship with Harry and his family, the crowded church filled with dignitaries, and my own feelings that I wasn't up to the task before me. I took a deep breathe, and this seemed to calm my nervousness.

"The Eulogy"

Dear family, Mr. President, Mr. Vice President, Public Officials, friends, and neighbors. Welcome to this celebration of Harry Smith's life. I don't know of anyone who more appropriately fits the prayer of our

Lords 23 Psalm. Harry was never afraid to combat evil. Those of you that knew him, knew this to be true. Harry gave up his life without hesitation in defense of his friend and President. This wasn't Harry's first act of bravery and heroism. His whole life was spent in defense of those threatened by something or someone. For me, Harry was my hero as far back as my first day on the school busfor kindergarten. Throughout my school days I can vividly recall the countless times that Harry was a positive influence on all of those he came in contact with. His presence made life a joy for all his friends. Everything just seemed to come together more smoothly when Harry participated. He was very smart, but never a braggart or bully, and always made you feel that you contributed to the solution of the problem. Harry was taken from us before his expected span of life. The reasons for the attempted assassination of our President remain unclear, but Harry's bravery and devotion to his friends are well known to all that knew him. If Harry had lived, his accomplishments would have been many. His death is a great loss to all. I will miss him. The President, and his country will miss him. His family and friends will miss him, but his influence and the memory of him and his lifes work will live on. We have lost our hero, but heaven has gained a new star. May God bless harry's soul, and his spirit. May God bless and comfort his wife and son. May God bless all of you that mourn his passing. The president has asked to say a few words for his very close friend, Harry. President Joe Cooper!

"Sally and John, my deepest sympathy goes out to you for your loss. Friends, citizens, I have a sense of guilt that it was an attempt on my life that was the cause of Harry's death. Fate does strange twists in our lives that we can't control. This country and I lost a dear friend. In honor of Harry's heroism, his wife and son will be presented the citizens medal of honor for his sacrifice to our country, posthumously. Thank you Harry. Thank you Sally and John. May God bless you and all of us that remain to carry on." As the President concluded his remarks and returned to his seat, I looked over to Jim Kelly with our predetermined signal, and he directed the ushers to escort Sally and John to pay their last respects to Harry in his open coffin. Sally bent over and kissed Harry, and I observed a tear fall to Harry. The procession of those in church then were ushered past the coffin. When the last of those in church had paid their respects, the funeral director closed the coffin, and placed our countries flag over the lid. The military honor guard then escorted the coffin to the hearse for the short ride to the cemetery. The funeral director with the assistance of his staff, gathered up the flowers to be given out at the cemetery. When all had left the church, I joined my wife, and the motorcade, for the trip to the cemetery. As I closed the church door, I felt a strange chill, even though the April weather was warm and sunny.

It only took a short time for all to arrive at the cemetery, because of its closeness to the church, even though the motorcade was the largest that our town had ever seen. The media was also there in full force. The burial site and vault were in place at Harry's family plot, waiting for the flagged draped coffin to be set in place. It took some time for the large crowd to assemble at the burial site, and when all was in readiness the military honor guard took up position on both sides of the flag draped coffin. I reached into my pocket for my bible, and recited the twenty third psalm. When I concluded this reading, the military honor guard gave the traditional gun salute, and then presented the flag to Harry's wife. Then at this point in the ceremony, Harry's wife and son went to the side of the coffin, and each placed a flower on the top of the coffin, As they were escorted away , the President went to the coffin, placed a flower on the coffin , and then gave a salute to his friend. All those in attendance walked past the coffin and placed a flower on the coffin, and gave a salute. The director, their staffs, and I were the last one's at the cemetery. They would stay at the site until the coffin was lowered and covered with earth. Jim Kelly came over to me and told me that as soon as the business here was finished, he would catch up with me at breakfast, and make sure that all would go smoothly. Josie had gone ahead to the breakfast with Sally and Karen. I watched for a while as the cemetery workers finished their task, and then walked over to my car, and unobserved, felt the tears slide down my cheeks. When I arrived at the breakfast site, there were security people everywhere, ready to assist everyone to their designated table. The number of people at the breakfast was much larger than those at the church. Jim Kelly once again exhibited his managerial skills. With his direction and guidance, he made sure that the imported caterer's seated and served all in attendance with the greatest skill and proper etiquette. Servers attended to each table in the most appropriate order, so that no one was slighted, and each table served simultaneously. The caterer's definitely knew their trade, and the successful manner that the breakfast was served proved this.

At Sally's and her son John's table sat the President, his wife Karen, his daughter Susan, and my wife Josie, and myself. At the tables to either side of ours sat the Vice President, and his group, and at the other table sat Harry's and Sally's parents, and the parents of the President and his wife. The conversation was casual because of the proximity of everyone. Joe Cooper did however indicate to me that there was much more for us to discuss in private. All through the breakfast the media was very busy making sure that they didn't miss a thing. At the conclusion of the breakfast the large crowds thinned out quickly after they had paid their final respects to Sally and her son John. Sally, John,

Karen and Susan then all left together. The President then took me aside to tell me that he would get in touch with me later in the day.

Josie and I along with Jim Kelly and his staff were still there as the caterers and other crews disassembled the tent, tables, and various serving stations required for the funeral breakfast. Jim told me that he would make sure that all would be cleaned up properly, and not to worry about anything. With this comment, Josie and I left for home. It was already two P.M. When we arrived at our front door. I looked around the church grounds and observed that everything had been cleaned up, and it looked like nothing had occured that morning. How strange, I thought. Life goes on.

It was about four P.M. When the President called on the phone, and asked if I could come to his house in about an hour. Of course, I said, and he told me that he would send a car to pick me up. Come alone, he said. At a quarter to the hour, the door bell rang, and I accompanied the driver to his car for the short trip to the Presidents local residence. My wife had an inquisitive look on her face as I left, but I told her not to worry, and I would return shortly. As we approached the Presidents house, I noticed that there were still quite a few media mobile car units near his home, possibly looking for a news scope. The secret service people ushered our car through the media, and soon I was at Joe's house. Joe and his wife greeted me at the front door, and Karen complimented me on the funeral service for Harry. I responded that the success of the proceedings was in great part due to the President's man, Jim Kelly. With these salutations completed, Joe and I went directly to his study. He told me that he was returning to Washington early Sunday morning, and that his staff had contacted my Bishop. The Bishop promised that a temporary replacement would be sent to my parish as soon as possible. He told me that Josie and I should be ready to go to Washington as soon as the replacement arrives. He would have Jim Kelly take care of all the logistics for our trip and stay in Washington, and for us not to worry about anything. I thanked him, and said that I was sure that Jim would handle everything expertly. With that out of the way, he then told me that he was sure that the conspiracy to assassinate him wasn't over. He wanted me to be very careful with my interviews and statements about this to anyone. Joe said that the secret service and F.B.I. Were handling the investigation, but he didn't know if he could trust either organization. Harry would have known how to get these agencies to do their job without instructions from the bureaucrats, he said. I said that I would try to think of what steps Harry would take to get to the bottom of this plot, and explore different scenarios. The obvious motive seems to be that your death would benefit the Vice President the most, just as you suspect. We know that he feels cheated by your political party for being passed over for the parties choice for the election. Joe said, we must be very careful not to alert him or anyone of our suspicions. I then told Joe that one of my parishioners was a retired naval intelligence officer, He is in his seventies, but still very sharp. Would you mind if I put some scenarios on the attempted assassination to him for his opinion. Joe said o.k., but don't let on who we suspect is at the bottom of this conspiracy. I told Joe that this man had been a friend to both our families for a long time. Joe asked what his name was, and I responded Tony Bridges, and the President said, oh yes, I remember him now. We talked for a short time, and then he sent for the agent to escort me back home. As we parted, he said that he would anxiously await my coming trip to Washington.

CHAPTER VIII
Invited to Washington

Sunday morning services were back to normal at the church. Thanks to Jim Kelly, our church and grounds bore no witness to the previous, hectic events of the past week. It felt good to resume the normal routine. During the sermon I told my parishioners that a substitute minister would take my place for a couple of months. I explained to them that the President had requested that I go to Washington for a short time to confer with him on some issues regarding the death out our mutual friend. Most of my parishioners knew of my close association with the President and Harry Smith, so it wasn't that unusual for them to hear why this was requested by the President. I explained that I wouldn't go until my replacement arrived. As I was giving my sermon I noticed that Tony Bridges was there with his wife. When he came up to the ront of the church to get the weekly news letters I whispered to him that I would like to see him at the conclusion of services.

The weather that Sunday was just as nice as the previous day when all of the activities of the funeral took place. After services I went to the front of the church to greet the parishioners as they departed. When Tony Bridges came by with his wife, I asked him if I could see him at his home in the afternoon. He said that it was fine, but I could see that he was puzzled at my request. I asked if three P.M. was satisfactory, and he said yes.

Josie and I left the church when all were gone, and went next door to our home. I turned on the television and Josie prepared our lunch. The news was redundant in its coverage of the previous days funeral services on the different networks, but there were little new news to report on the death of Harry, and the attempt on the President's life. At a quarter to three, I told Josie that I was going to Tony Bridges home to discuss some things with him. She asked what it was about, and I told her that I was interested in his opinion on the attempted assassination of the President because of his background in the Naval Intelligence Agency before his retirement. I could see that Josie wasn't quite satisfied with my response, and the intrigue of the events pertaining to all of this was starting to bother her. Our planned trip to Washington as a special adviser to the President was also troubling her. She asked me outright, just what kind of expertise I could offer the President on all of this investigation that more experienced and qualified advisers couldn't offer. My response was trust. I don't think that this satisfied her.

I drove over to Tony Bridges home, and as I pulled up to the curb, in front of his house, both he and his wife were tending their flower beds in this warm sunny April afternoon. After our greeting, He invited me to his rear yard where a gazebo was beckoning for us to sit. Tony asked if I preferred to go inside to his study. I told him that sitting in the gazebo would be fine. I looked around at the exquisitely groomed landscaping in his yard, and commented on how nice everything looked. He then drew my attention to the Spring flowers that were just beginning to bloom. I told him that it must have taken a lot of work to get everything to look so nice. He responded that both he and his wife enjoyed gardening, and since his retirement he had plenty of time for it. I then explained the reason for my visit. I told him that the authorities seem to be befuddled with the investigation on the attempted assassination and death of my friend. I asked Tony to give me some perspective, based on your background in Naval Intelligence, how this investigation should be conducted. Tony asked me why I thought the F.B.I. Wasn't performing accurately. I responded that I had no specific reason other than lack of any progress on their part. Tony knew of my close friendship with Harry and the President. And remarked how he remembered the three of us hanging around together when we were young boys, although he was older. Our small town left very little to the imagination, and most people knew everything that was going on, and who was doing what. As he was about to respond to my inquiry, I could almost sense the wheels of thought turning in his brain. He was sure that the F.B.I. And the Secret Service would most certainly look at all aspects of the case, but in my opinion, the first thing to be done is to identify the assailant. The autopsy must be done with the greatest of care and thoroughness so that any clue to his identity, his physical condition, and any indicators on what he did for a living could be determined. Once his identity is known, the next thing to investigate is a complete background check of his life, family, friends, finances, and political philosophies. The assailant must have known that he would be killed in this attempt, and knowing this, what would justify his going through with this. With D.N.A. Analysis, there may be clues to his nationality. With this complete check of his body, perhaps some clue as to why he would be willing to sacrifice his life might be learned. With all this information, perhaps the motive for this crime might be exposed. Tony said that he would start with this, and then move on to the motive for this crime. In any crime, the motive is always most important, and all those that would benefit most by the President's death must be on the short list of suspects. Knowing the President's instructions not to implicate the Vice President, I just nodded my understanding. Tony then concluded by saying that after his identity and motives are investigated, the telephone records, back statements, and travel movements can be checked which usually leads to the conspirators. Follow the money trail.

Tony's wife then joined us, and brought us lemonade. After some conversation about funeral proceedings conducted for Harry, and their beautiful landscaping, I thanked Tony for his insight on these tragic events, and bid my farewell. On the way back home, I wondered who the President could trust to carry out a proper investigation. When I arrived back home, Josie greeted me with the news that the Bishop had called, and that my substitute would arrive in town on the following Saturday. I would introduce my temporary replacement to my parishioners at next Sundays services. Josie and I would leave home for Washington during the week that followed. With this news, I placed a call to the contact given to me by the President, and informed him when we would be expected in Washington. About an hour after dinner that evening the President returned my call, and told me that plane tickets for our trip would be sent to the airport in Toledo, and accommodations for our stay in Washington at the White House would be taken care of by his staff. We would have to drive to Toledo to get our flight. With all these travel plans taken care of, Josie was in a quandary as to how much she should pack for our as yet unknown length of stay in Washington. I told her that we should pack the basics and if something more was needed we could purchase things in Washington. I reminded her that the President had told us that he would make sure that what ever was needed by us would be provided. This reassuring by me did very little to calm her nerves on the uncertainty of our mission. That following

Saturday, the Bishop, his Secretary, and the substitute minister arrived at our home in the early afternoon. After introductions, I brought my substitute , David Young to the guest room to deposit his luggage. We all then visited while Josie prepared dinner for our guests. The Bishop told me that the President had called him personally to request that he do all that he could to procure a substitute for me as quickly as he could. The Bishop then told me that David Young is just out of the seminary college, and is single. This is his first assignment, and I'm confident that he can handle his duties. His resume and recommendations are excellent. Josie called us to dinner and we had an opportunity to get to know David during the meal. After a pleasant dinner and conversation, the Bishop and his Secretary departed for their long drive home. David and I went over the sermon for tomorrow's church service that I wanted him to give after I introduced him to the parishioners. I could see that Josie also approved of our guest. It was almost like having a grown up son staying with us.

Sunday's sermon and introduction went very nice, and I felt confident that David would handle out church duties without any trouble. It was very nice having a young guest staying with us, and made both Josie and I wish that we had been blessed with children. That next Wednesday, Josie and I drove to Toledo to catch our flight to Washington.

CHAPTER IX
Our Trip

On arriving in Washington, we were met by two secret service agents who drove us to the White House. After we were driven past the multiple security check points, we left the car, and four other agents escorted us and our luggage to the suite of rooms provided for our stay in the Capital as guests of the President. Josie was quite impressed at the level of attention and fuss provided for us. A large bowl of fresh fruit was on the dining room table, and fresh cut flowers were placed on the entry sideboard. The agents escorting us, helped with our luggage, and a white house staff girl assisted Josie with unpacking. It was about one thirty P.M. when we finally got settled. A staff waitress brought us a lunch menu, knowing that we had not yet had anything to eat. The waitress told us that the President and his wife would dine with us at dinner, and that an agent would escort us to the Presidents room at six thirty P.M.. Both Josie and I ordered our lunch, and I'm sure Josie was as impressed as I with the red carpet treatment that we were receiving. After our lunch, we both took this opportunity to explore our guest accommodations. It was obvious to us that the President had given instructions to the White House staff to make sure that we were well taken care of. After exploring our rooms, we both were in need of a short nap to refresh ourselves from the hectic early morning of travel and excitement.

Now knowing exactly how to dress for dinner, we both put on our Sunday best for the dinner that awaited with the President. While we waited for the escort to take us to dinner, we watched the television news to see if there were any new developments in the assassination attempt. At six thirty exactly, there was a knock on our door, and we joined our escort to the President's private room. The President and his wife Karen greeted us as we entered. Josie and Karen both had smiles on their faces as we entered, and immediately hugged each other. Being sorority sisters from their college days, made them very comfortable with their relationship to each other. The President seemed very happy to see me, and first shook my hand warmly, and then gave me a hug. It was obvious that the President and his wife were in need of friends that they could trust, and be comfortable with. Joe directed us to the parlor, and called for the butler to take our order for cocktails. We engaged in small talk about our morning traveling, and the meeting with my Bishop and substitute, while we sipped our drinks. After a short while the butler told us that dinner was ready. We all went to the dining room, and were seated at a very elegantly set table. Josie asked Karen if her daughter Susan was at the White House. Karen explained that she was volunteering her services at a children's hospital in New Mexico with Harry's son John. Josie said that they would make a lovely couple, and Karen replied that she was hoping that they could carry on a courtship without any media harassment and political intrigue.

Our dinner was truly a gourmet experience and we both felt pampered by our hosts. After dinner and dessert, the butler brought port wine to finish our meal. Joe and I excused ourselves to the ladies, and went to his study so that he could bring me up to date on the latest developments. Josie and Karen went to the parlor to catch up on whatever it is that girls talk about. After the President told me of the very little progress on the investigation, I told him of my meeting with my parishioner, Tony Bridges. I related to Joe what I was told by Tony, on how the investigation should be conducted, and what was most important to learn. It was clear to both of us that little headway in the investigation was taking place. Joe said that with all the expertise, and the large number of government investigators looking into this, it seems that some new clues and developments should be learned. I told Joe that he needed a competent person who he could trust to take charge of the investigation. He responded that this was the problem. There is so much political intrigue and cliques around here that I don't know who I can trust. That's why you are here. I told Joe that someone out of the political loop, that hasn't established any alliances, and has demonstrated his thoroughness and ability could be selected. Joe asked, where do I find such a person. I responded that your young junior staff member, Jim Kelly, who I'm sure hasn't been involved with any of the Vice President's inner circle clique, would be an excellent choice. I can vouch for his thoroughness, and ability to get things done, and being Irish, I'm sure there must be a cop somewhere in his genetics and background. Joe looked at me and said, "see, that why I need you here with me." I then again went over all the recommendations on the investigation in great detail as they were given to me. I repeated that the first thing to do is to find out who this assassin is. I pointed out that Tony Bridges stressed that the autopsy should go way beyond the normal procedure, so that any clue, however small can be learned. After discussing this for quite a while, Joe and I left the study and joined the girls in the parlor. I could sense that the President felt a little better, and was happy that he had a trusted friend by his side. If only our friend Harry could also be here. When we three were together in our younger years no problem was insurmountable. We all four talked over old times for quite some time, and as it was getting late, Joe summoned a staff member to escort us to our room. On leaving, Joe said to me that he would summon Jim Kelly to meet with us on the following day. We were happy to get some rest as it had been a very long day of travel from our home in the early morning hours to a very exciting day at the White House. As we were getting ready for bed, Josie told me that Karen told her that Susan and John were seriously dating, and their engagement would be announced as soon as the proper period of mourning had elapsed. This news of their coming marriage was very happy for both of us. It was like having a part of Harry returned to us. It would be a year before they could let anyone know of this without causing raised eyebrows.

At seven A.M. The phone rang, and advised that room service would serve breakfast at eight A.M. If that was acceptable. With our approval given, we showered and dressed, and were ready when the maid came to our door with menus, Josie remarked that she could get used to this pampering without any difficulty. It was a short time after our order was taken that a beautiful breakfast was served. About nine A.M., the President called to tell that Jim Kelly had been summoned, and he would be at the Presidents office at ten A.M.. A staff member would be sent to escort me to the oval office. Karen would also like Josie to come and spend some time with her. We arrived at the Presidents office, and were greeted by both Joe and Karen. Josie and Karen then left us and went off to do their thing. The President called on the intercom to summon Jim Kelly. Jim entered the office with somewhat of a puzzled look on his face. He must have been wondering what was going on that brought him for his first visit to the Presidents office, being that his lower level of rank staffing would rarely bring him into personal contact with the President in his office. Our warm greeting to him seemed to put him at ease, and the President told him that on my recommendation, he was to be given a very important assignment as a special investigator and advisor to the President, and have his pay and clearance status raised to suit this new position. Joe then ask Jim if he was interested in taking this new position without being told what the assignment was. Jim said, "Of course I am, but excuse me if I look at bit dumbfounded at this offer." Joe then explained to Jim what he wanted him to do on the investigation of the assassination attempt. He listened intently as I also offered my recommendations as given to me by Tony Bridges. The President told him that he would report and answer only to him. When we were both finished giving him the scope of the job, Jim paused slightly, and then asked the President if he could bring two of his associates along on this assignment so that he would have trusted allies that he could depend on to be loyal. Without our telling him, he seemed to be aware that the reason that he was selected for this investigation was because the President felt there was a high level of conspiracy against him. Joe told him that he could bring as many associates along as he needed, all he had to do was ask, and they would be provided. " I repeat," said the President," you report and answer to no one but me." We then suggested that he start his investigation with the autopsy to make sure that it was extensive enough to learn as much as possible. I told Jim that he should search out another independent coroner to also conduct an autopsy to confirm the results. We must find out what was the nationality of the assassin, and if there were any other medical issues that the autopsy would discover that might provide a clue to his motive. With the business part of our meeting concluded, I asked Jim about his background before he was employed by the government. He told us that he was born and raised in Massachusetts, and went to City College there. He is the oldest of three children, with two sisters. His mother and father are retired and still live in Boston.I asked Jim what his college major was and he responded that it was police science, and it was his intention to be a cop like his father, until this civil service job opportunity came along. I turned to the President and said "I told you that there must be an Irish cop in his background". Joe chuckled, and said, "your hunch was right on." He then added that his grandfather was also a cop.

With the conclusion of our meeting, we all shook hands, and Jim was told to start immediately on his new assignment. As Jim left the office, the President made the necessary phone calls to give Jim the clearance and resources that he would need in his new assignment. The President then asked me to accompany him to his press conference where I would be introduced as his new special advisor. After the press conference Joe and I joined our wives for an unprecedented tour of the White House.

CHAPTER X

The Investigation

Jim Kelly lost no time in getting started with his investigation. With his level of classified clearance in the government established, he with the two aids that he brought along from his previous government job, started by going over the autopsy report. He immediately sought out the expertise to perform this task by hiring the services of a well known forensic scientist. With the backup of this expert at his side, he met with the coroner that had performed the autopsy on the assassin, and together they all went over all aspects of the report. They went over all the different tests to maintain the depth and complexity of each test. With the advice of Jim's expert, he instructed the coroner to re-do many of the tests, and perform them to a much higher degree of complexity. Jim also instructed the coroner to examine all tissues and organs of the assassins body completely, to see if there were any health issues that might give him a clue to this man's motive or identity. The original autopsy performed by the coroner seemed to follow the normal protocol and procedure. But also, seemed to stop short of the thoroughness required by the importance of this investigation. In my conversations with Jim on this matter we both decided not to do any finger pointing or make any direct accusations as to why an autopsy as important as this was done in such a cavalier manner. It was obvious that the assassin was Hispanic by his physical appearance. What was not known was if this man was most likely to be Mexican, Puerto Rican, Cuban, or from Central or South America. Further forensic tests would be needed to find out where the assassin came from. With the surveillance of Jim's expert looking on, additional blood, tissue, and D.N.A tests were taken. His body was examined for any indicator of what type of work that this man did for a living. The new subsequent data of this more extensive autopsy and examination revealed that the assassin was in his mid-fifties, and indicated that he had worked very hard during his life as as perhaps a farmer, laborer, or some other highly physical job. Then there was a new breakthrough in the examination. With more complete examination of his blood and organs it was revealed that the assassin was on extensive pain medication, and was diagnosed with pancreatic cancer. Jim's forensic scientist and the coroner both agreed that the assassin had approximately five months to live. This attempt on the President's life and the murder of my friend was apparently suicide by cop for hire. The next step in the investigation was to find out where the assassin came from, and try to identify him by looking for where he must have sought treatment for his disease, and then find out who hired him.

The tests to narrow down the assassins nationality were performed by conducting mitochondrial D.N.A. Analysis. These tests would narrow the trace to determine his probable ancestry, and Hispanic group. The equipment to perform some of these tests as called for by Jim's forensic scientist were not part of the coroners laboratory equipment, and had to be purchased by the government. This caused some delay in the process to find out the assassins nationality, but once these tests were conducted it was determined that his D.N.A. Markers indicated that he was Cuban. The Bio-analyzer equipment that was purchased, confirmed this. Jim now knew that the assassin was in his mid-fifties, was a farmer or laborer, was terminally ill with pancreatic cancer, and was most likely Cuban, Jim requested a meeting with the President to inform him of the progress in the investigation. The President made sure that I attended all of these meetings with Jim, when he gave the reports on his progress. At one of these meetings, Jim told us that a government official unknown to him had been nosing around the coroners office, and asking a lot of questions to the coroner and his staff. Jim took this man into custody and had his identity checked. It turned out that this intruder was a member of the Vice President's office managers staff. In Jim's interrogation of this man he wasn't able to learn why he was hanging around the coroners laboratory, and he released him with a warning to stay away from the coroners lab. When Jim told this in one of our meetings, the President didn't tell him of our suspicions that the Vice President was behind the plot to kill him. We would let only the evidence lead to the conspirators.

My normal routine at the White House was to accompany the President on his daily activities when requested to do so, and to offer my opinion when requested. We spent some time with our wives when there was a break from his Presidential duties. On one of these occasions while we were having lunch in the White House cafeteria with our wives, we were approached by the Vice President who was with his office manager. Her name was Carol Lawless, and was approximately the same age as all of us. We invited them to join us for lunch, Vice President, Andrew Walker seemed to be in a jovial mood as he introduced me to his office manager who I had not yet met. Andrew Walker complimented me on the funeral service that I conducted for Harry, and explained that he wasn't able to do this at the funeral. I thanked him, and told him that I was assisted by others who made everything turn out well. I thought to myself as we conversed, how clever he disguised his intent to do whatever it took to gain the presidency. Carol Lawless told the President that she was sorry for the incident at the coroners office with one of her staff, but assured him that it was just innocent curiousity. Andrew Walker then asked the President how the investigation was going, and who was conducting it. The President replied that he selected someone with a fresh outlook on the case as it seemed to be going nowhere. His name is Jim Kelly, and I have directed that he alone conduct it, and answer only to me. I think this somewhat terse response didn't sit well with the Vice President, judging by the look on his face. After that response, the Vice President had no more questions that he dared ask about the investigation. When lunch was over, and we parted company with the Vice President and his manager, the President said that Andrew Walker looked disturbed that the investigation has been taken over by someone who isn't part of his sphere of influence. I said that I also noticed that he didn't seem too happy with your response. Josie looked shocked when she heard this exchange between the President and I about the Vice President. She immediately asked me if we suspected the Vice President of any involvement with the assassination attempt. Prior to her hearing this exchange, I hadn't told her of our suspicions, but now that she heard this, we took her into our confidence, and swore her to secrecy.

Once it had been established that the assassin was probably Cuban, the search for his identity by Jim and his staff was undertaken by going to the Cuban Community in Florida. Their first task was to circulate a touched up photograph of the assassin, hiding the fact that he was deceased. The extensive circulation of this photograph bore no results. Their next alternative was to check every hospital in the state for all of the males diagnosed with pancreatic cancer in the last eight months. This was also very time consuming, and didn't give any help in the identification of the assassin. No hospital had given any male in our age group this diagnosis in this time period that was a match to our assassin. Jim met with us and requested permission to take his investigation to Cuba. There had been a long standing law prohibiting the travel of U.S. Citizens to Cuba, since the take-over by the communists. This meant that Jim and his two aids would have to go undercover. There would be no opportunity to circulate the assassins photograph without alerting the Cuban authorities of their investigation. Their investigation would have to concentrate on the hospitals for clues to the assassins identity. The President very reluctantly gave his permission for this, but suggested that a Cuban from Florida be hired to make the inquiries in the Cuban hospitals, and that they also hire a Canadian, posing as a tourist to be his contact man in Cuba, because it is common for Canadians to vacation there. Suggest that he bring his wife or girlfriend on this all expense paid vacation to facilitate the cover for his task. Jim agreed with the President's suggestion for the initial search of the hospital records, but said if we find out that the assassin is Cuban, it will be necessary for me to go to Cuba to gather additional evidence. The President concurred with this. Jim lost no time in selecting a Cuban and Canadian couple for this search. Once these hired agents were sent to Cuba to check the hospitals, they were able to positively identify the assassin. This process only took slightly less than a month. We now knew the assassins name. His name was Pedro Gonzales. This must be kept very secret, and our Canadian and Cuban operatives that were hired to obtain this information must not be told the significance of this man's name. When Jim brought this information to the President and I, and told us that it was now his intention to go to Cuba to verify these findings. Jim spoke a little Spanish, but not enough to conduct the necessary investigation. He would need to ask the Cuban American who was hired for the preliminary search to accompany him on this next phase. Jim along with this Cuban American, whose name was Vincente Gomez went to Canada, where he obtained forged identity documents that proclaimed them to be Canadian Citizens. This solved the language problem. Jim and Vincente then went to Cuba, posing as manufacturers of farming equipment sales agents. This cover would give them an excuse to travel in the rural areas. Their first stop was at the hospital where the assassin had been diagnosed with cancer, and they were able to bribe a clerk to get a copy of his records. With this information they were able to learn who the assassins next of kin were. Pedro Gonzales was survived by one daughter, and two grandchildren, a boy, and a girl. His wife had died two years ago, and his daughters husband had been seriously injured on their small farm about a year ago. His daughters name was Angela Posada. Jim's next stop was to get permission from the Cuban authorities to sell their farm tools. This wasn't an easy task, but finally their permit was granted. Jim and Vincente tried to rent a car for their countryside travels, but were forced to also hire a driver. The route planned for their sales trip would take them past the assassins daughter's farm. To keep their cover intact, they stopped at numerous farms along the way, and actually made a few sales. When they arrived at the farm once owned by Pedro Gonzales, and now owned by his daughter, they were quick to notice that they were living way above standards of all the poor farms that they had visited. Pedro's daughter, Angela, was a very pretty girl with two lovely children. Her husband's farm accident had made him an invalid, who wasn't able to help much on the farm. Angela was able to hire laborers to work on the farm, and maintain a high standard of living without any visible income. Where did that money come from. Jim made his sales pitch of the farm tools to start our meeting. He then had Vincente nonchalantly ask her about her father. They then revealed to her that her father was dead, but didn't tell her that he was an assassin. They offered to have the body returned to Cuba for burial, all expenses paid with the funds left by her father. They told her that he also left a sizeable amount of money that he wanted her to have. Vincente told Angela that he was a friend of her father, and was asked to make sure that she received this money on his death bed. He then asked her if she knew that he had cancer. She nodded yes. Jim asked Angela if she had a picture of her father. She went over to the mantel, and showed the picture to us. Jim took out his camera and snapped a picture of her father with the explanation that the bank holding her fathers funds required confirmation of his identity. They also require a D.N.A. sample and the name of your bank so that they can electronically deposit your inheritance. Angela looked puzzled at this request, and then asked if we were really farm tool salesmen. Vincente explained that we were and the lawyer representing your father's estate took advantage of the fact that I was your father's friend, and that I was scheduled to go to Cuba. This seemed to satisfy her. Jim had anticipated her reluctance to believe there cover story so he and Vincente were ready with a response. After some exchange in conversation, we drove back to our hotel, and prepared to travel back to Canada. The photo of Pedro Gonzales, and his daughters D.N.A. would be required for positive identification. It was Jim's intention to ask the President to make good on the promise to return her fathers body to Cuba and to send the fake inheritance money to her bank. All this was done to learn the name of her bank. With this knowledge, it was now possible to download all the information that we needed from her bank account to follow the money trail to see where this would lead. This could all be done back in the states with our computer experts. From Canada, Jim and Vincente returned to Washington where Jim told us of his progress, and request release of the assassins body for the return to his daughter, and the deposit of the inheritance funds to her bank account. Jim felt that there wasn't any need to let anyone know that the assassin had been identified. When and if this becomes necessary, it can be done later. The President was very pleased with Jim's progress, and gave the go-ahead for his requests.

The photo experts that Jim hired to compare the photo taken of the assassins body, and the picture that Jim took with his camera of Angela's father were analyzed by computer, and they confirmed that Pedro Gonzales and the assassin were the same person even though there was an age and health difference in the photos. The D.N.A. Sample of Angela positively confirmed that she was the assassins daughter. The computer hackers hired to invade her bank records discovered that a thirty thousand dollar deposit had been made to her account by her father a week before the assassination attempt on the President, and the murder of Harry. All this evidence now confirmed, the next step was to try to follow the money, and to see if we could determine who paid the money to the assassin. This phase of the investigation was going to be very difficult, and we must be very careful not to break the law in the gathering of evidence. Jim told us that he intended to check all of the expenditures of everyone on the Vice President's staff. The President gave his permission, but cautioned him to be very careful.

The motive for Pedro Gonzales to try to assassinate the President was clear. Knowing that he was terminally ill with cancer, and his daughter in trouble financially because of her husbands injury, he could easily be induced to attempt this crime, knowing he would most likely be killed. The conspirators were anticipating the use of just this type of individual who was terminally ill, and was desperate for money. Their plan was to search for this person in another country, to make it difficult to identify this hired assassin. As it turned out, they decided to choose Cuba to make it even more difficult to identify this person, because of the bad relations between our countries. To hire this person they had to send someone to Cuba. In our search for the conspirators we would try to find out who on the Vice President's staff had gone to Cuba from Canada, much the same as we did in our investigation. This search, plus following the money trail was our next step. Jim and his two aids brought the assassins body, and the fake inheritance money to Canada for shipment to the assassin's daughter in Cuba, While in Canada with the cooperation from the Canadian Government arranged by the President, they checked all the persons who had traveled to Cuba in the last four months. This was a tedious undertaking, but finally bore results. Jim was able to prove with security camera footage, fake passport records, testimony from Customs Officials, the identity of this person. It was the same person on the staff of the Vice President's office manager, Carol Lawless, who was nosing around the coroner's lab. We then sent Vincente back to Cuba with this man's photo to see if someone at the hospital, where Pedro Gonzales was treated could remember him. This was successful, and sworn testimony was given. Vincente then went to Angela's farm to see if she could also identify this person. Success there also, and testimony was given. Angela thanked Vincente for the shipment of her fathers body, and for the inheritance. She still wasn't told anything about her fathers involvement in the assassination attempt. Jim, his two aids, and Vincente all returned to Washington, and met with the President and I, to report on their progress, and present the evidence collected so far. The President seemed pleased with the results of their investigation, but seemed disturbed by the confrontation that was sure to follow. Jim's next step was the get a judge to issue a warrant for a search of the entire operating budget of the Vice President, and his staff, to follow the money trail of the funds given to the assassins daughter. The President needed time to think this over before he gave Jim permission to do this. The President told me that once this step is taken, Andrew Walker would know that we suspect him and his staff of the attempt on my life, and the death of Harry. There will be no turning back from this point. We have to give this careful thought before we proceed. I asked the President if there was a judge that he knew that could issue the warrant without letting anyone else in on our request. He said yes, but I still want time to mull this over in my head. I said perhaps Jim's computer expert can hack into these records without alerting the Vice President, and his staff. Jim said that he would check to see if this was possible. With that said, we concluded our meeting, but I could see that President Joe Cooper was very concerned.

When Jim Kelly caught one of the Vice Presidents staff snooping around the coroners laboratory he came to the conclusion that the conspirators were connected in some way to the Vice President. At one of our meetings after this incident he told the President of his suspicions. Without telling Jim that we also suspected that the Vice President was behind the plot to assassinate him, the President responded by telling Jim to let only the evidence find out who the guilty ones are. Without the President ever directly accusing the Vice President, the evidence was only pointing in that direction. We all felt that he was the mastermind behind this conspiracy, but we dare not make any accusations yet.

Jim contacted his computer expert, and asked him how much information he could gather by hacking into the Vice President's submitted budget reports without anyone knowing that this data had been taken. The computer expert replied that he could get the whole or any part of the report without anyone knowing that this was done. Jim swore this man to secrecy, and to do nothing until told. At our next meeting the President told us that he had thought about all the ramifications that accusing the Vice President of this murder and conspiracy would do to our country. This unprecedented crime will hurt our nation's reputation at home and abroad, but we cannot let it go unpunished. It is therefore my decision to proceed, and let the chips fall where they may.

Jim then told us about his meeting with the computer expert. The President gave him the go on this, but to do so with a warrant from the judge given to him by the President. Jim said that he with his two aids and his computer expert will check all the expenditures of all funds of everyone on the Vice President's staff, and all the travel comings and goings of each of them. All this investigating to be done very discretely with warrants from the judges selected only by the President. With this new task and avenue of investigation to be accomplished, Jim left our meeting. The President turned to me and said that you certainly picked the right man to carry out our search for Harry's killer. I knew that bringing you to Washington as my special advisor would get us to the bottom of this conspiracy.

It was about a week later that we three met again. Jim reported that he had succeeded in finding out who it was on the Vice President's staff who traveled to Cuba, recruited the assassin, met with the assassin's daughter, and deposited thirty thousand dollars into her bank account. All of this is proven with security camera pictures at airports, passport documents, at the hospital where the assassin was treated, at the bank where the money was deposited, and by financial records obtained by our computer expert. This is the same person who was caught snooping around the coroners lab., and who we found out previously had gone to Cuba by way of Canada. His name is Steve Sager. He reports directly to Carol Lawless. We have enough evidence to indict him for murder, and attempted murder, but unless we get him to incriminate any of his superiors on the staff of the Vice President, they will avoid prosecution. Jim added that we could also indict his immediate supervisor, Carol Lawless, and Steve Sager's co-staff workers, but unless one of them starts to squeal on the others, there isn't any chance of getting a conviction in a court of law on any of them. I suggested that the President select a judge that he trusted to issue a warrant for the arrest of Steve Sager, and see what happens when he is interrogated. Perhaps when he is shown how strong our case against him is, he might confess if offered a plea bargain for his testimony. Jim added that it might be a good idea to get arrest warrants for the entire staff of the Vice President, and see if any of them crack under the pressure, and give evidence. The President gave Jim the name of the judge to issue the arrest warrants, and to start by first arresting only Sager, and see where this leads, and then follow up with the arrest of the others. Maybe we will get lucky. The President then cautioned Jim to not use excessive force in any of this interrogation that could have this evidence thrown out in court. When this meeting ended, the President reminded Him to keep all these indictments as secret as possible, for as long as possible, so that the Vice President has little time to react.

CHAPTER XI

The Interrogation

With the arrest warrants secured, Jim met with a district supervisor of a nearby F.B.I. Office that was recommended by the President. His agent was known to be loyal to his country and to his duty as a Federal Agent. Two field agents were assigned to Him to assist him in the arrest of Steve Sager. Together they went to the Vice Presidents office , and with the arrest warrant in hand, made the arrest. This caught the Vice Presidents staff by complete surprise. Carol Lawless almost turned white with fear at this unexpected event. Steve Sager was handcuffed and read his Miranda Rights. They brought him to their district field office for interrogation. Jim led this suspected conspirator of the plot to kill the President, and the murder of my friend to a small interrogation room. The long ride from the V.P. staff office gave Sager time to restore calm to his initial nervousness and surprise arrest. Jim told him of our strong case against him, and told him that if he would cooperate with us, we could give him a plea bargain that would take the death penalty away. With his composure regained, and with a smug facial expression, he responded that that he wanted a lawyer, This didn't go as well as we had hoped. We then brought him to the holding center to await his arraignment. Steve Sager was single, had only one sibling, an older sister, and parents who were retired, and living in the mid west. It was two days later when he was brought to the Federal courthouse for his arraignment. He was represented by a high priced defense attorney, and pled not guilty. His attorney requested bail, but the prosecuting attorney convinced the judge to deny bail, and remand him to custody, based on the evidence, and the seriousness of the crime. Steve Sager was led out of the court house by two holding center guards, and brought to the waiting van for his trip back to the holding center. Jim was conferring with the prosecuting attorney when they got the news of the van being high jacked two blocks away from the courthouse, and the escape of Steve Sager. The large number of media who were representative of all the major networks, had been in the court room for the arraignment, were just about to leave when the news of the escape was announced. They all scrambled every which way for interviews with both attorneys and Jim to try to get a news scoop. Our attempts to proceed with the interrogation of Sager, and offer a plea bargain before the Vice President's staff could react, was a total failure. There wasn't any sense to get arrest warrants for the rest of the V.P. Staff, and no hope of any convictions of the conspirators without first convicting Steve Sager. Our job now was to find Sager, and return him to jail, and find out how he escaped. The Vice President, accompanied by the press, met with the President to profess his innocence of any plot by Sager. The President had always maintained a cordial front with the Vice President even though he felt that he was out to discredit his presidency. He did this for the sake of the country, and their political party, but at this turn of events, he told the Vice President that he was convinced that he encouraged or sanctioned this conspiracy. He then told him that he would do all in his power to have him impeached. With this direct accusation by the President, all pretense of friendliness was over, and the Vice President stormed out of the meeting in a huff. The press couldn't decide whether to question the President, or to rush out to report this news scoop. The press that tried to ask questions were put off by the statement, "no comment at this time".

Steve Sager's escape plan was put in motion by the denial of bail. If bail had been granted, it would have been the last that we ever would see him. When the van bringing him back to the holding center was only two blocks away from the court house, it was cut off by a large black S.U.V., and four gunmen forced the release of their prisoner. The guards were then knocked unconscious by the gunman, and they drove off. A bulletin for his arrest was immediately issued, and his picture was circulated on television on all networks. It was in the best interest of the conspirators that Steve Sager would never be heard from again. It was now Jim Kelly's task to apprehend him, and to interrogate him, and to convince him to accept a plea bargain, and to testify against those who were behind this conspiracy. This was no small task. The President called us together for an emergency meeting with the F.B.I. To discuss the best way to try for his recapture. It was Jim's suggestion that the most likely place that Sager would go was Canada, as this was where he had started out on his search for the assassin, he was familiar with the country, and how to obtain the false documents that he would need. From there he could search out the best place to go without ever being caught. No one had any better idea, so the President ordered the F.B.I. To assist Jim in the endeavor. Jim lost no time in setting this plan in motion, and was off to Canada with his two aids, and two teams of F.B.I. Agents. He split up the search into three teams, each with the responsibility of handling different aspects of the search. With the aid of the Canadian authorities, and wide circulation of Steve Sager's picture, and the reward as incentive, Sager was apprehended just before he was set to leave Canada for Argentina. The search of his luggage yielded a large amount of cash, and evidence of an offshore back account. Jim Kelly did it again. He guessed right. Sager was returned to the United States, this time under extremely heavy guard. The interrogation could now continue. When Sager was brought back to the holding center, and was being questioned, Jim told us that his attitude was more cooperative, and he expected him to confess and accept the plea bargain to save his life. He would be offered a sentence of thirty years with no parole, to be served at a Federal Prison that would offer good treatment for his testimony on his involvement in the plot to kill the President, and to testify against all others that were involved with him in this conspiracy. Steve Sager knew that his failure to escape was a death sentence by either a court trial or by the conspirators who had kept him from testifying. His only hope of survival was to accept the plea bargain offered by Jim Kelly. Jim accompanied the prosecuting attorney, his staff, and an attorney to represent Sager, brought the plea bargain for Sager to sign. The complete written testimony that followed gave the whole story of how this plot was started by Carol Lawless, and gave the names of all of her office staff who had a part in this conspiracy. It outlined in detail the part that each person played in the attempted assassination of the President. With this legal testimony obtained, Sager was sent off to a secret prison to await the court trial for the other conspirators, and hopefully the Vice President. All the conspirators got their orders and assignments from Carol Lawless, and the only connection to this plot by the Vice President would have to come from her testimony against him. If she failed to implicate him, it would be very difficult to charge and indict him. If she escapes, or is assassinated, the hope to bring him to justice would be lost. With the arrest warrants in hand, all the conspirators were rounded up, and put in custody. Special protective custody was arranged for Carol Lawless to make sure that nothing happened to her. All the conspirators in the office staff sang like birds when told of the evidence against them, hoping for leniency in their sentence, except Carol. She was tight lipped, and wouldn't cooperate, even when offered a plea bargain. The reason for this silence was soon given by the other office staff conspirators, and other staff workers who were not part of this plot. The Vice President and Carol were lovers, and had been having this secret affair for quite a long time, presumably without his wife's knowledge. All those indicted pled guilty, except Carol who pled not guilty at their arraignment. All attempts to persuade her to accept a plea bargain to implicate the Vice President in the conspiracy failed. When the Vice President's wife learned of his affair, she started divorce proceedings, and this seemed to solidify Carol's silence against her lover. With no hope of convincing her to change her mind, the trial date was set. The office staff members who were part of the plot, and had pled guilty were sentenced to twenty years in prison. Carol was denied bail, and was held for trial. The security that was provided for her, to make sure that nothing happened that would prevent her from being at her trial was increased. This would be an easy case for the prosecution with all the evidence that was given, but as long as Carol wouldn't turn on the Vice President, it could go no further.

The political allies that the Vice President had built up over the years of his career were now deserting him in droves. President Joe Cooper set in motion the procedure for impeachment of Vice President Andrew Walker, and with the V.P.'s loss of political influence, his impeachment was assured. The Vice President knew that he couldn't avoid impeachment, so he resigned as soon as these proceedings began. The media had a heyday with all these doings, and they made the most of it. The gossip about the V.P. And his affair with Carol Lawless, and the bits of news that somehow leaked out about the coming court trial of Carol Lawless were played out to there fullest extent. Even the smut magazines made the most of this scandal. The President was upset by this endless media over indulgence, but there was nothing that could be done to control it. We hoped that once the court trail was over that all this would end. To this end, the President did all he could to speed things up.

There was over three years left in President Joe Cooper's second term in office, and it was important that a new Vice President be appointed to fill out the term in office. The President had many meeting with his political party big wigs, and the powerful members of the Senate, and The House of Representatives to select this new V.P.. Finally, the person that Joe Cooper recommended was agreed upon by all. It was the Senator from the State of Virginia, Sam Watson.

He was the person that was originally considered to be Joe Cooper's running mate in his first term. Joe was very happy with this choice, as he felt sure that there wasn't any connection between him and Andrew Walker. Sam Watson was quickly sworn in as the new Vice President. With Andrew Walker out of the picture, and all of his obstructionist tactics over, the remaining things that the President and Harry wanted to accomplish became a reality. As these things were done, I could sense the pleasure that it gave Joe Cooper, knowing that together with his friend Harry, they had completed their task.

Josie and I had been in Washington for only a little over three months while all of this had taken place. It was the last week in July when I told the President that I felt that it was time for me to return to my church. It was apparent that I was no longer needed by the President, although he pleaded with me to stay. He told me that he would appoint me to a post as his special advisor. His offer was enticing, but I felt that I must return to Meadow Valley, and my congregation. The coming court trial for Carol Lawless was scheduled to take place in the beginning of August, and it was my desire to leave Washington before this started. With Joe Cooper's thanks and blessings, Josie and I made arrangements to return home. Karen begged Josie to try to convince me to accept the Presidents offer, and stay in Washington, but I knew that it was best for all that we return home. Karen and Josie had spent a great deal of time together during all this investigation, and it was nice that these sorority sisters had this time together, and hard for them to separate. Jim Kelly's success in his task, elevated him in President Joe Cooper's eyes, and he became an important part of the Presidents administration. Joe Cooper confided in me that he thought that this young man would go far in the Washington political arena, and he would use his influence to help him along the way. Jim Kelly had yet to complete one task in this special advisory position to the President on this investigation, interrogation, and trial to bring the guilty to justice. He would finish this task as a special court room advisor to the prosecuting attorney. At the conclusion of the trial, the President told me that he intended to appoint him as his personal advisor. Former Vice President, Andrew Walker was still in Washington, and was frequently visiting Carol Lawless in the holding center along with her high priced defense attorney, who was being paid by Walker. Walker's ex wife had agreed to a large cash settlement, and their divorce was finalized. She left Washington very quickly to try to avoid the harassment of the media. Andrew Walker had amassed a large fortune during his long political career, but these recent events were costing him dearly.

As the day came for our departure from Washington, both Josie and I made our sad goodbyes to the President and his wife, to Jim Kelly and his staff, and to all the White House staff that had been so good to us during our stay. We were taken to the airport for our flight home, and met at Toledo by my replacement, Reverend David Young, for the drive home to our church. He seemed very pleased to see us, and was full of questions about all the intriguing news of the attempted assassination of the President, the murder of Harry, the investigation of the perpetrators, and coming trial. All these events had been covered by the media, and I wondered what they would talk about once this was over. Everything at St. Paul's had gone smoothly, and David had done an excellent job in my absence. David would stay on as my aid for the time being, until he would be assigned his own parish. It was nice to have David staying with us. Both Josie and I were growing very fond of this young man. It was like having a son that we were never blessed with . It was about a couple of days after we returned home that Josie received a letter from Karen, telling her of the yet to be announced wedding plans of her daughter Susan, and Harry's son John.

CHAPTER XII

The Court Trial

It was the first week in August, and the weather in
Meadow Valley was beautiful, not too hot, just right.
I was nice to get back to my duties at the church.
David had done an excellent job in my absence, and
I decided to have him conduct the Sunday service so
that he would find the experience necessary for the
time when he would be given his own parish. We had
only one service on Sundays at St. Paul's. The other
weekly duties at our parish were done together. Josie
was in frequent contact with Karen in Washington,
and was kept abreast of the latest news on the
upcoming court trial of Carol Lawless. The media
was having a heyday with all of the trial gossip and
the alleged love affair between Carol and the ex Vice
President, Andrew Walker. The trial was scheduled
to start in a week. The hype build up by the media
wasn't their classiest moment, and was embarrassing
our country with its circus like coverage.

The trial began with the selection of the jury. The
prosecution and the defense each questioned those
citizens called to serve at this trial, with the idea of
selecting only those that would be most favorable
to their case. It was at this part of the trial that the
Judge had to close the court to the media because
of their lack of courtroom decorum. It was also at
this point that the Judge also instructed the bailiff to
make arrangements for the court room visitors to be

admitted by pass, to be obtained from the attorneys for the prosecution and the defense, and the federal court. The poor behavior of those at the jury selection, was the cause of this response by the presiding judge. After the twelve jury member and alternates were selected, the trial was adjourned to the following day. The three major networks plus fox cable were each allowed a court reporter, and a sketch artist, and a recording device. This ended the court room circus.

This trial was to determine the guilt or innocence of Carol Lawless only. All the other conspirators indicted had pled guilty and accepted a plea bargain, but were required to give testimony at the trial. The trial began with opening arguments given by the prosecution and the defense. The very expensive defense attorney for Carol was being paid for by Andrew Walker. Walker was a lawyer, and was allowed to assist the defense attorney in the court room. He had considerable wealth, and the amount of his political power that he retained was unknown. Jim Kelly was scheduled to give testimony at some point, but at the insistence of the President, was allowed to sit with the prosecuting attorney and his staff. The defense attorney, Walker, and the defendant, Carol Lawless, were all impeccably groomed in very business attire. It was obvious that Carol was getting special preferential treatment in the holding center. The opening statements by the court, and the opening arguments by the attorneys, brought the time close to the lunch hour, so the judge adjourned the trial to continue after lunch. The media made sure that even the smallest details of the trial were reported each night in the evening network television news, and in all the newspapers the next day. As the trial continued after lunch, the prosecution called Steve Sager to take the stand, and give testimony as their first witness. The prosecuting attorney asked Sager to tell the jury the whole story from beginning to end of his involvement in the attempted assassination of the President and the murder of Harry Smith. He began his testimony by telling the court that his position in the V.P.'s staff office was an assistant and advisor to Carol Lawless, the office manager, and answerable to no one but her, and the Vice President. He then told the court that it was her that at first suggested that he could gain power and wealth if he could get rid of the President. When she saw that I was compatible with her suggestion, she told me to figure out a plan to assassinate the President. It was common knowledge in the office that Carol, and the V.P. Were lovers, and that they have been having this affair for a very long time. It was my assumption that he knew of this conspiracy, but I never spoke to him about it. After I came up with this plan, she approved it, and complimented me on the ingenuity of using a foreigner who was terminally ill to kill the President. This assassin knew that he would die in this attempt, but was willing to do this for the money that his daughter needed to save their home.

Carol then told me to have the office staff provide me with the assistance I required, but to only let those know of my plans that I could safely include in the conspiracy, and assure them that they would be richly rewarded. The prosecuting attorney then told Sager to give the names of all those who were part of the conspiracy, and to tell what part they played.

At the end of the prosecution testimony, the defense attorney started his cross examination by asking Sager if any of his co-conspirators in the office were witness to any of this planning to assassinate the President between you and Carol Lawless. He responded, "no", and then the defense attorney said, "then it's only your word that she was involved with this plot." He then asked Sager if the plea bargain offered by the prosecution, took the death penalty away from his sentence. Sager answered "Yes". The defense said, "no further questions, but reserve the right to recall the witness".

The prosecution then called each, and everyone of the office staff indicted and took their testimony, and then the defense put the same question about their plea bargains, and if they could incriminate Carol Lawless. They all responded, "no". The remainder of the Vice Presidents office staff who were not charged in the conspiracy were called to testify. The prosecution was able to get all of who were indicted, and those we were unindicted, who gave testimony to state that they were sure that Steve Sager was acting directly under the orders of Carol Lawless. The judge adjourned the trial for the next day.

As everyone was getting ready to leave the court room, Jim Kelly approached the prosecuting attorney, and asked him how he felt the first day of testimony went. The look of the prosecutor's face gave the answer before he could respond. He told Jim that so far the testimony has presented the jury with a reasonable doubt that Steve Sager was acting under the orders of Carol Lawless. It's very important that we convince the jury that these two acted together in this crime. Jim said that this was also his impression.

Day two of the trial began with the prosecuting attorney calling the remainder of the office staff who were not indicted, to testify. One by one, they all testified that they were sure that Carol and Sager acted together. On cross examination, the defense attorney asked them if they could offer proof that they acted together. Again, they all said no except the very last one to take the stand. She responded "yes". The judge, the attorneys, the jury, and all those in the courtroom were eager to hear the evidence that would link the two together in the attempted assassination of the President, and the murder of Harry Smith. This office staff clerks name was Sandy Martin. The defense attorney then tried to rebuke her statement by saying, "you mean you think you can prove it".

No, Sandy said," I can prove it." At this response the defense attorney was forced to let her continue her testimony. She said that there is a security camera in the office that I purposely adjusted the direction to point at the glass partition between the general office and the office managers office. I did this one night at quitting time when I was alone in the office, so that I would have proof of the two of them talking together. This cameras pictures will show Carol's face and lips as she talked with Sager. A lip reader should be able to tell what she is saying. That's my proof. I did this because I suspected that something very bad was going on between the two of them. At the end of this statement the prosecuting attorney asked the judge if he could approach the bench. The judge said yes, and told the defense attorney to also approach the bench, The prosecutor asked the judge to give a recess, so that the F.B.I. Accompanied by Jim Kelly could immediately go to the staff office to secure this camera and picture footage before this important evidence disappears. The judge granted the recess, and the F.B.I. secured the camera.

A lip reading specialist was then obtained to analyze the camera footage of Carol talking to Sager. Her analysis was all that the prosecution needed to convince the jury of Carol's involvement and guilt. The trial resumed and this evidence was presented. The prosecution then rested their case. The defense attempted to rebut this evidence with their own expert, but it was apparent that the jury didn't buy it. After a long list of character witnesses, the defense rested their case. The judge then adjourned the trial to the next day for closing statements by the attorneys. These statements took the entire day, and at their end, the jury was cloistered to give their deliberation on the verdict. The only thing that could be done now, was to wait for the verdict, and hope that the jury finds her guilty. The prosecution, the defense, the media, and the defendant, Carol Lawless along with her alleged lover, Andrew Walker, waited restlessly for the outcome to be announced. It became apparent that there would be no verdict this day, so the judge adjourned court, and all would be called to return to court when the jury had made their decision. They jury had been sequestered for two days before everyone was called back to court to hear the verdict. When all were present in court, the judge asked the jury foreman if they had reached a verdict. There were three possibilities. Guilty, Not guilty, or were unable to reach a unanimous agreement. Everyone in the court room listened with bated breath. The foreman responded "yes your honor", and gave the verdict to the judge. The judge looked at the verdict, and then gave it back to the foreman, The judge then asked the jury foreman, "how do you find". The foreman said, "Guilty as charged". The hear-to-for quiet court room was transformed into excited exuberance. The judge called for quiet, struck his gavel, and proclaimed that the trial was concluded. Andrew Walker was hugging Carol Lawless who was crying, as the bailiff took her into custody. Jim Kelly and the prosecuting attorney shook hands as the congratulated each other on the outcome. The media was in a rush to report the news. That evening on the television, all the major networks were speculating on the sentence that was yet to be announced at sentencing. At sentencing, she was given twenty five years to life for her crime. Andrew Walker still had enough political power to see that the federal prison that she would be incarcerated in was one of the more elite. As the year went by the media lost interest in news concerning Carol Lawless and Andrew Walker who had escaped any punishment for his part in this conspiracy, and still retained his enormous wealth, and still had sizeable political influence. President Joe Cooper and I were disappointed that Walker wasn't punished for the death of our friend Harry, but we both were certain that his punishment would come from God.

CHAPTER XIII
The Wedding

It was the end of Spring in the second year of Joe Cooper's second term as President, when the wedding invitation came in the mail for the July wedding of Susan Cooper, and John Smith. Josie had been corresponding frequently with Karen and Sally, so this invitation came as no surprise. The wedding was to take place on July 24th at the suburban estate of Joe Cooper's home on the outskirts of our town. I had been previously asked to perform the nuptials for the marriage which would be performed at Joe Cooper's home. This would eliminate the travel time between the church and the reception which followed the marriage ceremony. Joe Cooper still had a year and a half left in his second term in office. The media talked about the candidates to succeed him in office was starting to "rev" up. Joe Cooper's political party, with Joe Cooper's approval, were favoring Vice President Sam Watson, who took over as V.P. When Andrew Walker was forced to resign. Sam Watson was in his mid sixties, and had a long and unblemished public career as first congressman, and then Senator of the state of Virginia. Joe and Sam were very compatible, and worked well together. With Joe Cooper's successful leadership in resolving the nations recession in his first term, and with his continued guidance in his second term, his political influence was at an all time high. With Joe's support, Sam Watson was a shoe-in to receive his parties nomination. The president was also pushing along the career of his advisor, Jim Kelly, who had performed so diligently.

Then unexpectedly, the Secretary of labor was killed in a car accident. Joe appointed Jim to fill this cabinet post. Joe confided in me during one of our many private communications, that he was going to push hard for Jim to be selected as the nominee for Vice President on Sam Watson's ticket. With Sam's approval, and Joe's political power, this was most likely to happen.

The early days of Summer seemed to fly by as the wedding day got closer. Josie was asked by Karen and Sally to participate in the planning for the wedding. It was Susan's and John's wish that the wedding be held at her parent's estate near town. All other plans she left up to her mother. The three sorority sisters seemed to be in their seventh heaven with these plans. While I observed these preparations taking place, my thoughts went back to the first day that when we all three of us met on that school bus. Who could predict that three young lads who met on that bus, would have such a great impact on our nation, and someday have their offspring become united in marriage. The joys and sadness that life holds are mystifying. To think that such a small town like Meadow Valley could play this role in this huge nation is unimaginable. As the wedding day came closer, the communications between the girls increased tremendously. The girls had no Jim Kelly to handle the logistics, but they seemed to handle the preparations without any problem. The marriage of a sitting presidents daughter at their home estate would require solutions for many problems that other similar social functions don't have. The need for security for the President at an event like this, poses many unique problems. They were responsible for the Presidents protection, no matter what the occasion. The extensive grounds of the Presidents estate would require careful scrutiny. Karen with the help of John's mother Sally, and my wife Josie, supported by professional caterers, landscapers, and numerous other social event experts, made all the preparations for a very lavish wedding ceremony, and the reception. Large tents were set up at dining areas, for protection in case of inclement weather. A chapel like gazebo was constructed for the exchange of wedding vows. Decorative canopies, serving stations, band stand and dance floor set up along the side of one area, beautifully set tables and place settings for the guests, overhead lanterns and flower decorations everywhere, and seating on both sides of a carpeted isle in front of the chapel, all were ready for the coming ceremony. Caterers were hired for the wedding cake, food service, and beverage service.

Those standing up in the wedding for Susan and John were their sorority and fraternity friends from college. Overnight accommodations for all guests that required this were provided.

As the day of the wedding approached, the preparations started to intensify. Meadow Valley had never experienced a social event of this magnitude. On the Friday before the Saturday wedding, rehearsal was held at Saint Paul's Church. Following rehearsal, all were invited to Sally's suburban home for the traditional rehearsal party. Sally and her son John were beaming, and I felt glad that their remorse about Harry's death was eased by the coming event. I don't know why, but I suddenly had the feeling that things were going too smooth. I have never been much of a physic. I somehow felt uneasy. I went over to the Secret Service guard on duty, and asked him if they had completed their security preparations for the wedding. He said that everything was under control. This somehow didn't satisfy my concern.

Saturday morning arrived after a restless night of worry. Josie, my assistant, David Young, and I were up early. After a light breakfast, we all groomed and dressed for the wedding. David would assist at the ceremony. The wedding was scheduled to take place at 11A.M.. What luck! The weather was warm and sunny. It was about a ten minute drive to Joe's home. At Josie's insistence, we left our home at 9:30. She joined Karen and Sally to see if they required help on any last minute detail. David and I went over to the garden chapel constructed for the ceremony, to make sure that all was ready. Flowers, seating for guests, ushers waiting for guests to be seated, were all in place. I looked around the perimeter of the estate and noticed the Secret Service security trying to look innocuous. One of our parishioners who played our church organ was commissioned to play the wedding march on an organ that had been brought on site for this occasion. At about 10:30, the ushers started to seat the guests. Soon John arrived with his fraternity brothers who were standing up for him. I asked John if he had the wedding ring. He reached into his pocket, and gave it to his best man, to be returned at the proper moment in the ceremony. I looked around at all the smiling faces. The aura of happiness was everywhere. I was alone with my apprehension that all was not well. I buried these thoughts, lest they spoil the happy atmosphere.

At the appointed time, all was ready. The men in the wedding party joined the beautifully gowned girls down the carpeted aisle to the altar. They were followed by the flower girl, and at the rear of the aisle the organist started playing the wedding march. And one by one the men escorted the girls down the aisle. Then the bride and her father Joe Cooper followed. I then performed the nuptials, and pronounced John and Susan, man and wife. The guests then erupted in joyous cheers and congratulations. At that moment my fears of tragedy were gone.

The reception that immediately followed the wedding ceremony was wonderful. The food, the drinks, the music, the dancing, the conversation, were an event that wouldn't be forgotten. A photographer that was hired for the occasion took numerous pictures. I happened to notice the Secret Service roust a group of paparazzi at the perimeter of the grounds, away from the property. The guest list included many of the president's political friends, including the Vice President and his wife. Jim Kelly was there with his just announced fiance. Her name was Sandy Martin. She was the girl that had secured our criminal case against Carol Lawless. As the afternoon passed, and the bride and groom left on their honeymoon, the guests started to slowly depart. I felt relief that my fears of tragedy were unfounded. At that moment I thought of my friend Harry. If he were above, how proud he would be to witness this marriage.

I walked over to Joe. He took my arm and directed me to join him at one of the canopied beverage bars. He wanted to join with me in the toast to our friend Harry. Apparently we were both thinking of him at the same moment. As we raised our glasses to Harry, A silent thud passed through Joe's body and then through mine. I was conscious just long enough to see the red blood appear on Joe's white tuxedo shirt, before we both collapsed to the ground.

CHAPTER XIV

Between life and Death

I felt no pain or concept of body. Below on a hospital gurney lay a man being attended to by numerous staff. The patients face was covered by an oxygen mask. Numerous tubes and medical devices were attached to his body. Suddenly a doctor called for a defibrillator to be used on the patient below. Stand clear he shouted and zapped the man with an electrical charge. Again he zapped the man. The doctor removed the oxygen mask to listen for a sign of life at the mans mouth. At this moment the man's face was exposed, and I realized that the man on the gurney was me. I was experiencing an out of body sensation. My attention was drawn above to a beckoning light at the far end of a tunnel like visual field. At the far end of the tunnel, someone was waving to me, and calling me by name to come forward. As I advanced, I recognized that it was a young boy calling for me. It was my friend Harry, As I got nearer to him, he suddenly motioned for me to stop. In a voice that I remember was Harry's, he said go back, it's not yet your time.

I opened my eyes, and felt my hand being held by my wife Josie. I was in a patient bed in a private hospital room. As Josie noticed that I was awake, she whispered, thank you Dear God. I observed tears of thanks leave her eyes. I smiled at her, and asked her how long I had been here. She told me that I had been in coma for a week, and that the operation that I had, saved my life. At that moment I remembered that I was having a drink with Joe Cooper when we were shot. I asked Josie about the President. The Doctors were able to save him, she said. He was as bad off as you, but is going to be ok. Both of you are going to need a long time to fully recover.

I asked Josie, who shot us, "we were shot, right". Yes she said, by the same bullet that passed through the President, went through you. Both of you are very lucky to be alive. Did they catch the assassin, I asked. Yes, you will never guess who it was, she responded. It was Andrew Walker. He was killed by the Secret Service in an exchange of gunfire. I told Josie that his need for revenge must have overwhelmed his senses.

It was two weeks later when we were released from the hospital. Joe went to his home outside of our town, and I returned to my home. My assistant, David Young would assume all duties of running Saint Paul's church. The President would turn over the power of the presidency to the Vice President, Sam Watson, until he was able to resume his duties. The doctors told both of us that our recovery would take a long time.

When we were shot, I was too sick to witness the constant media coverage of this latest assassination attempt on the President. They exposed every sordid detail of the ex V.P.'s love affair with Carol Lawless, and his crazed need for revenge against Joe Cooper, who he blamed for the loss of the presidency, and all of his misfortune since.

I was still too weak to do much, but it felt good to be out of the hospital and home. I had no problem with the inactivity of my convalescing at home, but Joe Cooper was having trouble dealing with it. In our phone conversations, he indicated that he was anxious to get back to Washington and resume his duties. Josie, Karen and Sally were all in town together, and seemed to be enjoying each others company. Susan and John returned to town from their honeymoon when they heard of the shooting, but now had resumed their planned trip, and career search. The days passed quickly, and the Thanksgiving holiday was near. Josie, David and I were invited to Joe's home for the holiday dinner. Sally, Susan and John were also there. It was very nice to be together, and we had much to be thankful for. At the end of dinner, I told everyone that I wanted to finish the toast to Harry that was interrupted when Joe and I were shot. We all raised our glasses to our departed friend. It was then that I told everyone at the dinner of my out of body experience, and my encounter with the tunnel like corridor with bright light at it's far end. I then told them of seeing Harry. I explained that this out of body sensation was caused by death and revival with the defibrillator I told everyone that I just had to let them know of this experience. Everyone seemed glad that I shared my encounter with the other side.

Joe and Karen remained in town for the Christmas holiday, but after the New Year, they returned to Washington, and Joe resumed his presidency. It was a very happy holiday season with all of us being there together for the celebration of Christmas.

CHAPTER XV

Back in Washington

When the President returned to the White House, he assembled all the necessary officials to resume his presidency, including the Chief Justice of the Supreme Court, and Vice President Sam Watson, who was acting President during the Presidents recovery. Sam Watson fulfilled his duties of the presidency with honor and integrity while acting President. His every action indicated that he would make an excellent president. Joe Cooper alwaus got along extremely well with Sam, and were compatible in their political philosophy. It was because of this that Joe selected Sam to fill the term of Vice President when Andrew Walker resigned, and why he was supporting him to be the parties choice for President in the coming election in November. Now that Sam was relieved of his acting presidential duties, he was free to campaign in the numerous state primaries. This final year of Joe Cooper's term in office would give him just enough time to complete the legislation on the remaining reforms that he and Harry sponsored that brought the country out of the recession. Joe would leave office with the knowledge that his term in office was a success.

Jim Kelly had performed his duties as Secretary of Labor with skill and ingenuity, and his political stock was on the rise. The President was backing him to be Vice President on the ticket with Sam Watson. The good relationship between Joe and Sam would help with this, but the selection of V.P. Would have to wait for political convention results to be completed. The convention was scheduled to take place at the end of June. The final word on the selection of the V.P. Would have to be made by the nominee for president. If Sam got the nomination for President, it looked good for Jim, as Sam liked his enthusiasm and ideals. Joe felt that the country would prosper if Sam Watson and Jim Kelly were elected in November.

The Winter and Spring of Joe's last year in office passed without incident. The convention was held, and Sam Watson was confirmed to be their parties candidate for President. He selected Jim Kelly to be his running mate as Vice President. They were very busy with their campaign, and both were out of Washington for most of the time. The media was focused on the coming election, and the attention was off of the lame duck President. The election came, and Sam Watson, and Jim Kelly, defeated their opponents, and were elected to the Presidency.

It was about a week after the election that there was breaking news. Carol Lawless had escaped from prison. When she had been been convicted for her part in the assassination attempt, and the murder of Harry, Andrew Walker still had enough political power and influence, that he was able to have her incarcerated in one of the select prisons. Her escape would have never happened at a more secure facility.

She was no where to be found. She had vanished. The F.B.I. Had a nation wide hunt for her. The Secret Service guarding the President was well aware of the hatred that she felt for Joe Cooper. In her twisted mind, he was the cause for the death of her deceased lover, Andrew Walker, and for her conviction, and incarceration for murder, and attempted murder. The F.B.I. Felt that she had access to as many funds and resources as she needed to remain in hiding for as long as she needed. The Secret Service suspected that she was highly motivated to seek revenge on the President, and to possibly try for another attempt on his life. She felt that her lover, Andrew Walker, and her were so close to having it all, the presidency, marriage to Walker, and unlimited power, that all her failures were Joe Cooper's fault.

President Joe Cooper, and his wife Karen, left Washington, and returned to home in Meadow Valley for the Christmas holidays. The inauguration for the new president was scheduled for January 20, in Washington. Joe would return to the Capital, after the New Year holiday, for his last few days in office, and be there for the inauguration ceremonies for the new president, and Vice President. The Secret Service was on their guard, and watchful for any threat during this time.

Inauguration day arrived. The new President, Sam Watson, would take the oath of office from the Chief Justice of the Supreme Court. This oath would be given on the steps in front of the Capital building. A podium was set up for this oath. In attendance were Senators, Congressmen, Government Officials, and dignitaries of many countries. The Plaza in front of the Capital building was packed with a very large crowd, gathered there to witness the event. The security was everywhere, and everyone was aware of their presence. As time for the oath drew near, one of the Secret Service agents checking the crowd spotted Carol Lawless. The disguise of a wig that she was wearing, only drew more attention to her, and was noticed by the agent. She was in a large group of people, and appeared to be holding some type of detonator. The agent called for backup, and informed their supervisor that she seemed to have a large bulge under her coat. She seemed to be inching her way closer to the podium. On the advice of the lead Secret Service agent, a tranquilizer gun was obtained, as she continued getting closer to the podium where the President, the President elect, and the Supreme Court Justice stood. She still seemed to not notice that she was being observed. When in position, the agent fired a dart at Carol, and she fell unconscious. Strapped to her body, under her coat were enough explosives to kill hundreds, including both the President, and the President elect, and the others at the podium. She was willing to end her life in suicide, to achieve her goal of revenge. Her incarceration this time would not allow any chance of escape. Only a limited number in the audience were aware of what happened, but that was enough for the media to find out, and they would be covering the news for some time.

The inauguration then continued without further incident. After Sam Watson took the oath of office from the Chief Justice, it was Jim Kelly's turn, and he became the youngest Vice President in our U.S. History. Standing by his side, when he took the oath was his new fiance, Sandy Martin. Jim and Sandy started dating after the court trial of Carol Lawless. The media was in a frenzy with questions about the suicide bombing attempt, and not knowing who the suicide bomber was, only made them all the more persistent. Finally, after all the handshakes, and congratulations the dignitaries at the capital steps started to leave, and the crowd in the plaza started to disperse. Joe Cooper and his wife remained in Washington for all the inauguration events, and the new Presidents, state of the union address, and then returned to his home in Meadow Valley. It was around the middle of February, just before Carol Lawless was scheduled to leave prison for her trip to court, to be indicted for her new crimes, that the media interrupted the television programming with breaking news. Carol Lawless had hanged herself in her jail cell. The evil doers and their crimes had come full circle. That next Sunday in my sermon, I stressed the point that the fruit of crime and evil is an eternity in bitter hell. The assassins that killed my friend, and attempted murder, now get their just rewards.

The month of April came, and the fourth anniversary of Harry's death was near. We all happened to be in town, so we decided to gather at his burial site, to pay our respects on that day. Sally, her son John and his wife Susan, Joe and Karen, Josie and myself, all assembled to pray and pay homage to our departed friend. As we gathered around his tombstone, my thought went to the tunnel of light calling for me. Joe looked at me, and seemed to know what I was thinking of. We both then said in unison, "We don't know when, but the three amigos will be together again."

THE END